The Case of the Disappearing Deejay

"Dan Wildman is the greatest deejay in the world," Bess declared. She, George, and Nancy were listening to the radio during a picnic dinner.

The song ended, and there was a long silence. Then a loud crash came from the radio. The girls could hear grunts and groans and the sounds of objects falling to the floor.

Bess laughed. "Dan the Wild Man is always doing something crazy," she told her friends.

"Maybe it isn't a joke," Nancy said.

Then as suddenly as it started, the sounds of the struggle stopped. After a brief, tense silence, one word came out over the air. It was muffled, but there was no mistaking what word Dan had cried.

"Help!"

Nancy Drew
Mystery Stories

Available from MINSTREL Books

NANCY DREW MYSTERY STORIES®

NANCY DREW®

THE CASE OF THE DISAPPEARING DEEJAY

CAROLYN KEENE

A
MINSTREL®
BOOK

PUBLISHED BY POCKET BOOKS

New York   London   Toronto   Sydney   Tokyo   Singapore

This novel is a work of fiction. Names, characters, places and incidents are products of the author's imagination or are used fictitiously. Any resemblance to actual events or locales or persons, living or dead, is entirely coincidental.

A MINSTREL PAPERBACK *ORIGINAL*

 A Minstrel Book published by
POCKET BOOKS, a division of Simon & Schuster Inc.
1230 Avenue of the Americas, New York, NY 10020

ISBN 0-671-66314-3

First Minstrel Books printing June 1989

10 9 8 7 6 5 4

Cover art by Aleta Jenks

Printed in the U.S.A.

Contents

1

Dinner with a Deejay

"Turn up the volume, Bess," Nancy Drew said, grinning. "I really like Dan Wildman."

"The Wild Man," Bess Marvin said. "What a name! He's the best deejay ever!" She held a ketchup bottle over her hamburger and slapped it across the bottom.

It was a warm, clear evening in early summer. Nancy Drew and her friends Bess Marvin and George Fayne were enjoying a cookout on the patio of the Drews' backyard. Nancy had told them to wear their jeans and come for a relaxing evening of hamburgers and croquet.

Bess was still trying to get some ketchup out of the bottle, so Nancy reached across the picnic table and turned a knob on top of her portable radio and cassette player. She tucked a strand of reddish blond hair behind her ear and winked at George sitting next to her.

"What's so great about Dan Wildman?" Nancy egged Bess on.

"Are you kidding?" Bess said, lowering the ketchup bottle and blinking wide blue eyes at Nancy. "He's the best thing that's ever happened to KRCK! He's funny, he's talented, he's hip, he's . . . he's . . ."

"Incredibly good-looking," her tall, slim, dark-haired cousin George prompted.

Bess looked surprised. "What?"

"Isn't that what you said when you showed me Dan Wildman's picture on that billboard last week? 'He's sooo incredibly good-looking?' Black hair, blue eyes, dimple—"

Bess blushed. "Well, yes, but—"

Nancy smiled. "I get it."

"But I'd still think he was *talented* even if he weren't . . . somewhat cute," Bess said, running fingers through her long, straw blond hair. "But the fact that he *does* happen to have a rather handsome face doesn't hurt."

George winked back at Nancy. "Just like I said—'incredibly good-looking,'" she said, grinning.

"Shh!" Bess said, waving at her cousin to be quiet. "I want to hear what he's saying."

"—and that's it, kids!" Dan Wildman's husky

2

voice was saying. "You're tuned in to Dan the Wild Man on KRCK, the River Heights radio station where things are jumpin', where rock is pumpin', where blues we're dumpin'!" The girls laughed at the crazy rhyme.

"Stay with me, now," Dan said. "We've got the hottest music right here on K-Rock from six till nine, so don't you go away."

A commercial for a local car dealership came on then, and Bess took a bite out of her hamburger. "He's always talking in rhymes," she said. "I love his energy. I wonder what he's like in person?"

"Probably all tired out," George teased. "I bet he goes home and turns into a sloppy puddle of Jell-O."

Nancy smiled. "I like Dan Wildman, too," she admitted. "But there's another deejay at KRCK who I like just as well."

George snapped her fingers. "Rockin' Ray Ludlow! He's my favorite."

"Yes," Nancy agreed. "He *is* good. Both Dan and Ray play great rock 'n' roll."

"Oh, but Ray's been at KRCK for *ages,*" protested Bess.

"Ray has a lot more experience than the Wild Man," said George. "And obviously the station owner agrees with me. Rockin' Ray has the top time slot on the air, from nine P.M. to midnight. That's when most of the kids listen in."

"He won't have it for long," Bess said. "Mark my words, Dan the Wild Man will take over that spot soon."

"You may be right," said Nancy. "He's the deejay all the kids talk about."

The backdoor opened. "Who's ready for strawberry pie?" a voice called out.

"I know I am, Hannah," Nancy called back. "What about you, Bess?" she added, her blue eyes twinkling.

"Are you kidding?" replied Bess. She grinned at the Drews' housekeeper, who was crossing the patio toward the girls. "I'll wreck my diet any day for one of your strawberry pies, Hannah."

Nancy and George smiled at each other. Bess was slightly plump, and she was always on a diet. But staying on a diet wasn't easy for Bess.

Hannah set the pink-and-white-swirled pie down in front of Bess.

"That's dangerous, Hannah," George teased. "If you put that pie down right in front of Bess, she'll probably inhale the entire thing before any of us get a piece."

Hannah laughed. "Now, I know she'll do no such thing." She smiled fondly at Nancy. "I just thought I'd make one of Nancy's favorite pies since she doesn't happen to be working on a mystery at the moment. I knew she'd have time to enjoy it. Sometimes when she's busy on a case, I hardly see her."

Hannah Gruen had been like a mother to Nancy since the death of Nancy's own mother fifteen years before. Nancy was only three at the time Hannah came to live with the Drews, and Nancy and her father couldn't imagine life without her. Hannah worried about Nancy's work as a detective but was proud of her ability to help people and solve difficult—and sometimes dangerous—cases.

Nancy laughed. "I guess you're right, Hannah," she said. "Sometimes I get so involved with a case that I forget to eat."

Bess's eyes got big. "You *forget* to eat? That would never happen to me!" She watched Hannah's hand as she made the first cut in the pie. "Make mine just a teeny bit bigger, okay?" she said.

Dan the Wild Man's voice rang out. "And now, here's one from the request line."

The girls turned their attention to the radio on the end of the picnic table. "Susan says she cares for Tim; in fact, she says she's right for him. So, listen, Tim, this song is new; and Susan's sending it out to you."

The girls laughed.

"Now he's got his radio audience making up those dumb rhymes," George said. "I have to hand it to him, he really does have a following."

"Oh, all that rock 'n' roll sounds the same to me," Hannah said, handing a piece of pie to Bess.

5

"That's what my grandmother says," Bess said. "But Mom and Dad kind of like rock music."

While the song played on the radio, the girls ate their dessert.

Hannah sat down at the picnic table and cut herself a piece of pie.

"Dan Wildman is the greatest deejay in the world," Bess said. She licked the tip of her fork with her tongue and stared dreamily into the distance. "I wish I could meet him."

George rolled her eyes. "Dream on," she said. "He probably has bodyguards to beat off all of the adoring fans who follow him around."

"No, he doesn't," Bess said. "I saw him at the movies yesterday. He was there alone."

"I can't believe you didn't try to get his autograph," Nancy said with a smile.

"Neither can I," said George. "Then you could have seen those blue eyes and that dimple up close and personal."

Bess sighed. "I know," she said. "I guess I was just feeling too shy."

The song ended, and there was a long silence over the air. Bess leaned closer to the radio. "What happened to the sound, Nancy?"

Nancy adjusted the knob. "Nothing."

Just then a loud crash came from the radio.

"Good grief!" Hannah said. "What was that?"

Bess laughed. "Hannah, you have to get used to Dan the Wild Man. He's always doing something crazy. Last week, he brought his neighbor's dog into the studio and put him on the air. He swore the dog could say Wild Man, and he tried to get him to talk all afternoon. It was a riot!"

The girls all leaned close to the radio now, waiting to hear more. They could hear grunts and groans and the sounds of objects falling to the floor.

"What's he doing this time?" Hannah said. "It sounds like a struggle."

Bess rolled her eyes. "It's just a gag, believe me, Hannah. I'm not falling for any more of Dan Wildman's put-ons."

More grunts were heard.

"It certainly sounds realistic," Hannah said, frowning.

"Yes, it does," Nancy agreed. "I don't get his joke."

"Neither do I," said George.

Nancy turned to face George. "Maybe it isn't a joke," she said.

"Of course it is!" Bess said. "Just wait, he'll explain it all in a minute."

The sounds of a struggle continued, and everyone gathered closer to the radio.

"This seems more serious than most of his jokes," Nancy said. "Usually you know right away that Dan is up to one of his tricks."

"It's weird, all right," Bess said.

Then as suddenly as it started, the sounds of

7

the struggle stopped. There was a brief, tense silence as the women leaned closer to the radio.

Then one word came out over the air. It was muffled, but there was no mistaking what word Dan had cried.

"HELP!"

2

Where Is the Wild Man?

"Dan Wildman's in trouble!" cried Bess. "Nancy, what should we do?"

Nancy stood up quickly. "I think we should get over to the station right away. Maybe we can help him. But we've got to hurry!"

Moments later, Nancy, Bess, and George were flying down the road toward the radio station in Nancy's blue sports car.

Hannah had feebly protested their leaving with a comment about the pie going to waste, but she knew that there was no stopping Nancy when there was a mystery to investigate. Bess had managed to say, "Keep that piece for me, Hannah," before being dragged away by her friends.

The girls tuned in to **KRCK** on the car radio while they sped toward the station. The radio station continued to be quiet for a while, then a prerecorded sports report came on the air.

"That prerecorded report proves it's not one of Wildman's jokes," George said. "He'd never stay off the air this long."

Pulling into the station parking lot, Nancy counted four black-and-white police cars. Another was just arriving. The police officer who was driving it jumped out and ran into the station.

"Something awful must have happened," Bess said. "I've never seen so many police cars."

The station lot was filled. Nancy parked the car as close as she could to the one-story brick building. The girls hurried up the sidewalk and through the station's heavy wooden door.

They found themselves in the front lobby. It was buzzing with activity. Several uniformed police officers stood in front of a reception desk, talking to a short, attractive blond woman. She held a tissue in her hand and talked very quickly, gesturing in small, nervous movements. Another officer disappeared around the corner and down a hallway. Two men dressed in business suits entered the lobby from the hallway and pulled out small notebooks. They wore police badges on their lapels.

"Police detectives," said Nancy. "This is really serious."

One of the detectives spotted Nancy and her friends and strode over to them.

Nancy saw him coming and spoke first. "We're here to see Dan Wildman," she said confidently. Experience had taught her that it was necessary to speak up calmly but forcefully during her investigations. All too often, she had to deal with people in positions of authority who assumed she was nothing more than a curious teenager.

The detective, a tall, handsome man with gray hair, looked at her seriously. "Dan Wildman has been kidnapped," he said.

"Oh, no!" exclaimed Bess.

"What happened?" Nancy asked.

"No one saw it happen," he answered. "Apparently, Wildman was broadcasting as usual and someone barged in and took him by force." The detective nodded down the hall toward the broadcast booth. "The kidnapper—or kidnappers—left a note saying further instructions would follow."

Nancy nodded. "We heard a scuffle on the air." She met the man's gaze. "May I see the note from the kidnappers?"

The detective's eyes narrowed. "Why?" he asked. "What's your business here?" He took out a pencil and gazed at each of their faces, as if to memorize their features. "What are your names?"

"I'm Nancy Drew," Nancy said. "And these are my friends George Fayne and Bess Marvin."

The detective wrote their names into his notebook.

"Nancy's a famous detective," Bess piped up. "You mean you haven't heard of her?"

"If you'll call Chief McGinnis of the River Heights Police Department, he'll vouch for me," Nancy said, hurrying on. "Call him if you need to check me out. But he'll tell you I'm okay. Now if you don't mind . . ." Nancy started to walk around him, but the detective stepped forward to block her.

"This is police business, Ms. Drew," he said. "You can't go back there. I *will* check you out, believe me, but no matter who you turn out to be, I won't let you get in the way and mess up an investigation."

A woman's voice interrupted the detective. "Excuse me, did I hear you say that you're Nancy Drew?"

Nancy and the girls turned to see the short, blond woman they'd seen when they first arrived. She stood next to the detective. The worried look in the woman's eyes softened momentarily.

"Are you Nancy Drew, the young detective I've read so much about in the papers?"

Nancy modestly admitted that she was that person.

The woman extended her hand. "I'm a big

admirer of yours, Nancy," she said. "I'm Helena Santos, the station manager."

Ms. Santos faced the detective. "I'd like Nancy and her friends to stay." She turned back to Nancy. "Would you join the investigation? I'd be so grateful for any help you could give us."

The detective shook his head and walked away.

"I'd be glad to help," Nancy said, smiling. "We were listening to Dan when it happened. He's one of our favorite deejays."

"He's certainly popular with our listening audience," Helena said. Her eyes filled again with worry. "I can't imagine who would do such a thing. Poor Dan. I just hope that he's not hurt."

Nancy touched the woman's arm. "We'll find him," she said. "Don't worry."

"Thank you," Ms. Santos said. "Dan's not only an asset to the station, but we like him very much. Most of us, anyway." She smiled faintly. "I'm not quite old enough to be his mother, but sometimes I feel like mothering Dan. He's so . . . well, young and enthusiastic. Sometimes I have to rein him in a little. His ideas for his show can get a little too crazy, so I asked him to consult me about his program ideas."

Nancy spoke up. "You said, 'most of us' like him. Does he have any enemies that you know about?"

Helena Santos thought a moment before answering. "Well, Dan is a real professional and very ambitious. There are some people at the station who don't care for him and think he's pretty stuck on himself. But I think those people are jealous of him. He's a really nice guy and just wonderful on the air."

"You can say that again!" Bess said. "He obviously enjoys being a deejay. I don't think he could fake that enthusiasm."

Nancy spoke up. "Ms. Santos—"

"Please call me Helena," she said and smiled.

"Thank you," Nancy said. "Helena, you mentioned that some people are envious of Dan."

"Yes," she said. "But I can't imagine that anyone *here* could've had anything to do with his kidnapping, if that's what you're thinking."

"And no one saw what happened tonight?"

"No. I was in Neal Graham's office—"

"Who is Neal Graham?" Nancy asked.

"Oh, of course you wouldn't know that," Helena said, and smiled apologetically. "Neal is the owner of KRCK." Nancy nodded. "I was in his office filing my daily report. I always do that just before I leave for the day. And no one else was in or near the broadcast booth, either. We just suddenly realized that no one was on the air."

"How did you find out?" Nancy asked her.

"Our engineer, Tom Cottner, came running in here to tell me," she said.

"May I talk to him?" Nancy asked.

14

"Of course," Helena said. "Come with me."

She led the girls out of the lobby and down the hallway. She pointed to a window along the wall.

"That's the announcer's booth," she said. "Dan was on the air in there when he was kidnapped."

The girls peered through the glass into a small, crowded room. It didn't look big enough to hold more than five or six people comfortably. Right now, the booth was filled with police officers and detectives.

"I'd like to stop back here later," Nancy said.

"We will," Helena said.

She stopped at a closed door at the end of the hall.

"I think Tom's in the lounge," she said, nodding at the door. She pushed the door open and they entered.

The lounge was small. It held five small, round chrome-and-plastic tables and three vending machines that dispensed soft drinks and a variety of junk food. A sink and counter took up one short wall.

A small, heavyset, dark-haired man sat at a table next to the soda machine. He held a cigarette in one hand and a diet soda in the other. He looked up as the women approached.

"Ladies, I'd like you to meet Tom Cottner, our engineer. Tom, this is Nancy Drew, George Fayne, and Bess Marvin."

Tom stood up and nodded to the girls. He addressed Nancy with the faintest hint of a sneer. "Oh, right, the famous girl detective." He took a drag on his cigarette.

Helena spoke up, her voice firm. "Tom, I've asked Nancy to help in the investigation. Please give her any help you can."

Cottner shrugged. "Sure."

Nancy smiled politely. "Mind if I ask a few questions?"

He looked at her directly and folded his arms. "Why not? But I already told the police everything I know. Which isn't much."

Helena said, "Let's all sit down. It isn't very fancy in here, but I think we'll be more comfortable sitting."

They sat down at Tom's table, and Nancy asked, "Where were you just before you realized that Dan wasn't on the air?"

Tom pointed to a spot on the table in front of him. "I was sitting right here taking my break," he said. "That *is* allowed, you know, taking a break after four hours of work."

Helena shot him a warning glance. "Careful, Tom," she said.

Nancy wasn't fazed by Tom's rudeness. She'd seen it before in people who didn't feel comfortable with a young woman still in her teens who was joining an important criminal investigation.

16

Nancy continued her questioning. "What happened after your break?"

Tom squashed his cigarette in the ashtray in front of him. "I went back to the announcer's booth," he said, "and it was empty. Except that there were signs of a struggle: a pair of earphones, the program log, papers, and carts, scattered all over the floor."

George spoke up. "Carts?"

"A lot of music we play is on cartridges— 'carts' for short. The deejay lines them up on the table next to him in the order in which he plans to play them." He paused. "They were all over the floor."

"Were you the one who found the kidnapper's note?" Nancy asked.

"Yeah," Tom said, shifting uneasily in his chair. "It was propped up on the console."

"Is that the panel with all the switches and dials?" Bess asked. "We saw it through the window in the hall. Is that where the deejays sit?"

Tom sneered. "Yeah."

Nancy turned to Helena. "May I see that note?"

"Surely," Helena said. She rose from her seat. "I left it in my office. I have to give it back to the police, though. They'll need it as evidence." She glanced at Tom a moment and said, "Nancy, girls, come with me."

17

When they were out of the lounge, Helena apologized for the engineer's rudeness. "I don't know why he acted that way," she said. "I know that he likes Dan very much. I'd think he would want to help you."

Nancy smiled. "He's probably just upset about the kidnapping," she said. But she wondered if there was any other reason why Tom Cottner was so hostile.

Helena led them to her office at the end of the hall. She handed the kidnapper's note to Nancy.

Nancy turned the paper over in her hand. "Just standard white typing paper."

Nancy read the typed note aloud. " 'We've got the Wild Man. Instructions later. Follow them carefully if you want to see him again.' "

She looked at the note closely. "Look at this," she said. Everyone gathered around her. Nancy pointed to each of the typed *n*'s on the paper. There were five of them. "Look at how the letter *n* slants just slightly to the right."

Bess groaned. "A clue if I ever saw one. And what do you bet that some poor soul will have to run around typing on every typewriter in River Heights in order to find the one whose type matches this note?"

George grinned. "Sounds like a good job for *you*, Bess."

"Terrific," Bess said, rolling her eyes. "I can't wait."

"Can you make a copy of this note for me?" Nancy asked Helena.

The older woman nodded. "I'll do it right now. There's a copier just down the hall."

A few moments later, Helena was back with a copy of the kidnapper's note. She handed it to Nancy and said, "I think the police are out of the announcer's booth now. Would you like to see it?"

"Yes," all three girls replied.

"I want to see where my favorite deejays play all that great rock 'n' roll!" Bess said.

"Right now, we're just playing nonstop music and the advertisements and sports reports that were scheduled for this evening," she explained, as they headed back down the hall. "I tried to get in touch with Ray Ludlow soon after the kidnapping, but he wasn't home. I wanted him to take over the rest of Dan's show." Helena glanced at her watch. "It's nearly eight o'clock. If Ray didn't get my message, he'll probably show up at two minutes to nine. That's his usual style."

They came to the door with the window next to it. Helena pushed the door open and they walked in.

The room was crammed with electronic equipment, the broadcast console taking up most of the room. Just as Bess had described, it was loaded with dials and levers.

"It looks like the front panel of an airplane!"

Bess said. "What are all these knobs and switches for?"

Helena smiled. "They're used for a lot of different things," she said. "Some control the volume of the different tape players, some are for recording or playing back phone calls or the news feed that comes in every hour."

Suddenly her face brightened. "Hey, I just realized something." She pointed to a large tape deck standing in the corner of the room. "We may have another clue, Nancy. This tape deck runs constantly every day, taping everything that goes out over the air. That means we have a recording of the kidnapping!"

Helena ran the tape back, found the spot she was looking for, and hit the play button.

Once again, the girls heard the sounds of the struggle that they'd listened to from Nancy's backyard. And at the end came Dan's muffled plea for help.

Bess shivered. "It was bad enough the first time."

"May I have a copy of that tape, Helena?" Nancy asked. "I may need to hear it again later."

"Certainly," she said. "I'll make one for you and another copy for the police."

Just then, several people ran past the window that looked out over the hall.

"What's going on?" George asked.

"Let's find out," Helena said, reaching for the door handle.

It didn't take long to pinpoint the source of the commotion. A loud, angry voice bellowed from the lobby. "What's going on here? I was just pulled away from a very important meeting with our advertisers! Give me the whole story, and I want it *now!*"

"Uh-oh," Helena said. "That's Neal Graham, the station owner. He's . . . well, he's not known for his gentle manner."

The girls hurried along behind Helena into the lobby. A short, balding man with a mustache was surrounded by a half dozen people, all of them talking at once.

"Where's Helena?" he yelled over their heads. "You people get out of my way! I can't hear myself think with all of you jabbering at me."

Helena approached the man quickly and put her hand gently on his arm.

"Neal," she said. "I'm glad you're here."

"What's going on?" he thundered. "Did I hear right? Dan Wildman was kidnapped *on the air?*"

"Yes," Helena said. "The police arrived right away, and we're conducting an investigation."

It was only then that Neal Graham noticed Nancy, Bess, and George. His eyes widened. "*We're* conducting an investigation? Who are these kids?" he growled.

21

Helena turned to the girls. "This is George Fayne, Bess Marvin, and *this*," she said importantly, "is Nancy Drew. I'm sure you've read about her success in solving mysteries. Ladies, this is Mr. Neal Graham, the owner of KRCK."

The girls nodded and Neal Graham frowned at Helena. "This is serious business, Helena," he said. "We don't need an amateur detective getting in the way. We'll let the police handle it."

Helena started to protest. "But, Neal, Nancy is—"

"I don't want to hear about teenage detectives! I want to hear about Dan Wildman!" he interrupted angrily. "How did it happen? Where was everybody?"

Helena quickly filled him in with all the information she knew about the kidnapping and showed him the note from the kidnappers.

"The uniformed officers have left, but the two plainclothes detectives are still here questioning people," she added.

Nancy had been watching Graham closely ever since they'd found him in the lobby. Surely, she thought, he would be concerned about the well-being of his employee. But if Graham *were* concerned about Dan Wildman, he certainly wasn't showing it.

Graham angrily faced Helena. "I should've known. Wildman is unprofessional—I knew he'd get the station in hot water. I never should have

22

hired him in the first place." Graham began pacing back and forth. He ran the palm of his hand over the top of his head. "At least he's out of my way for a while, anyway." He stopped, turned to Helena, and jabbed the air with an index finger. "But when this thing is over, I'm going to fire him!"

Nancy glanced at George and Bess. They looked as shocked as she was.

"But, Neal, Dan is an excellent deejay! Except for Ray Ludlow, he has more fans than all of the others combined," Helena said.

Just then, over the public address system, a voice boomed out.

"And now, we're going to play some *really* special music here on KRCK," the voice said.

Helena looked over her shoulder toward the announcer's booth. "Who's on the air?" she said. "That's not Ray's voice."

"This music is a tribute to a terrific deejay here at KRCK, Dan the Wild Man," the voice said. "We love him here at the station. So, folks, sit back and listen. This is coming at you from DBF, Dan's Biggest Fan!"

Neal was so angry that his face turned deep red and a vein on his temple stood out, snaking around the side of his head.

"Who in thunder is *that?*" he roared. "Who is Dan's Biggest Fan?"

3

Lenny Gribble

Nancy and her friends raced down the hall after Neal Graham and Helena Santos and stopped at the window of the announcer's booth.

A skinny young man who looked to be in his late teens sat at the broadcast console. He slid a cartridge into the panel in front of him and pushed the button to start it playing. He turned to the window, grinned, and waved at the five faces staring in at him.

Helena gasped. "Lenny Gribble!"

Neal Graham glanced angrily over his shoulder at Helena. "Did you tell this kid to go on the air?"

"Of course not," she said. "We just hired him a few months ago. He's still learning—"

That was all Neal Graham needed to hear. He

burst into the announcer's booth, grabbed the surprised young man by his shirt collar, and dragged him out into the hall.

"Who told you to take over here?" Graham yelled.

"Uh, no one," Lenny said, squirming. "I just thought——"

"Well, you're through," Graham roared. "You're fired! Get out!" He released Lenny's shirt and turned to see Tom Cottner strolling up the hall from the lounge. "Cottner, get on the phone to Ray Ludlow. Get him in here. We need someone on the air. NOW!"

Tom Cottner nodded and hurried into the nearest office. Lenny started to leave.

"Please stay for a moment," Helena said to the young man. Then she faced Neal Graham and said softly, "Neal, I understand why you're so angry with Lenny. He had no right to put himself on the air. But he auditioned and I hired him to substitute and eventually have a regular show. He's good. He really is. Why not give him a chance to do what I hired him to do?"

"Absolutely not," Graham said. The deep red had faded from his face. Helena had succeeded in calming him down somewhat, but he was still obviously angry about Dan's kidnapping and Lenny's impromptu tribute.

"That's all I need," Graham continued. "Another employee making decisions and acting on

25

them without consulting anyone. No wonder there's chaos around here. No, Tom Cottner will get hold of Ray and he can take over."

"But I already tried to get Ray on the phone," Helena said. "He's not at home."

"Helena," Nancy said, glancing at her meaningfully. "Will you play the tape of the kidnapping for me again? I'm sure Mr. Graham would like to hear it, and maybe it will give us some new information."

Helena quickly agreed, realizing that Nancy's request was a play to distract Neal Graham from firing Lenny. She and the girls returned to the announcer's booth with Graham. The station owner waited impatiently while Helena rewound the tape of Dan Wildman's kidnapping.

Nancy had another reason for having Helena play the tape. She wanted to watch Neal Graham's face as he listened. Could he possibly have been the kidnapper? He certainly didn't seem to care what happened to Dan Wildman, his own employee!

But the tape played, and Graham's face gave nothing away. Then, halfway through the playing of the tape, he turned toward Nancy and happened to catch her watching him.

Once again, his face turned red. "What is this!" he said, his voice rising in anger again. "You were watching my reaction, weren't you, young lady? Is that why you wanted to hear the tape? Is that how you *amateurs* find out who's guilty when a crime is committed?" Sarcastically, he raised the pitch of his voice to sound like a young woman's. "Forget about evidence and proof, let's just watch his face. Then we'll know who kidnapped Dan the Wild Man."

Nancy was speechless. Graham snorted angrily and stormed out of the announcer's booth and down the hall.

As they moved into the hall, Nancy noticed that the color had drained from Helena's face. The woman turned to Lenny. "I'd like you to continue your broadcast for the time being," Helena said. Lenny started to protest, but she interrupted him. "I'll take full responsibility," she said. "Stay until Ray Ludlow gets here." Lenny nodded and, smiling faintly, disappeared back into the announcer's booth.

Helena turned to the girls. "Nancy, I don't know what to say," she said. "If I had known how rudely you would be treated here, I'd never have asked you to stay and help. I'm really sorry."

Nancy squeezed her arm. "It's all right, Helena."

Bess spoke up. "Is Mr. Graham always this cheerful?" she asked. "It must be delightful to see that guy every day."

Helena forced a smile. "He's not easy to get along with normally," she said. "But lately, he's had some pretty serious financial problems that have made him—well, pretty bad-tempered, as you can see."

"That's a shame," Nancy said.

They moved along the hallway.

"Don't feel sorry for him, Nancy," Bess said. "He acted like a total jerk."

"I don't think you should have to put up with that kind of treatment," George agreed.

"We're here to help Helena," Nancy reminded her friends. "And Dan Wildman."

"The poor guy," Bess said with a sigh.

"How do Dan and Ray Ludlow get along?" Nancy asked Helena. "It seems that they're each other's toughest competition."

"That's true," Helena said as they moved into the lobby. "More so lately. Dan is really developing a strong following with the young people in River Heights. I'm afraid that Ray is feeling more and more threatened by Dan. Those kids who are tuning Dan in used to be Ray's biggest fans."

Nancy frowned. "You know, with Dan having such a large listening audience, I would think that Neal Graham would be pleased to have him working at KRCK. Dan is definitely an asset to the radio station. But it was pretty obvious that Neal Graham wasn't very worried about him."

Helena nodded. "I know." She sighed deeply. "Neal realizes how talented Dan is. And he knows that Dan is good for business. Lately, we've gotten more advertising during Dan's show, because his audience has been growing. But, you see, Ray Ludlow is an old friend of Neal's. I think it bothers him to see Dan moving in on Ray. As I said before, Dan is very ambitious and would love to take over Ray's top night spot. But Neal won't ever give it to Dan. Not while Ray is working here."

"Do *you* hire the employees at the station?" Nancy asked.

"Yes, I do, but Neal has the final say. Oh, that reminds me," Helena said nearly under her breath. She took several quick steps to the reception desk and grabbed a pencil and a piece of paper. "Let me write this down before I forget." She scribbled a minute, then put the paper in her pocket. "I need to place an ad for a production intern," she explained. "With all the trouble this evening, I'd nearly forgotten."

"So you did hire Dan Wildman?" Nancy asked.

"That's the crazy thing about this," Helena said. "I hired him, but it was at Neal's insistence! He heard Dan's audition tape and interviewed him and was impressed with the very qualities that are now making Dan so popular: his wit, his drive, his imagination. I guess it didn't occur to Neal at the time that Dan could become so popular that he'd become a challenge to his friend, Ray Ludlow."

"Are you Ms. Santos?" a voice interrupted. The girls looked over to the reception desk where one of the plainclothes detectives was seated. He held up the telephone receiver, his hand covering the mouthpiece.

Helena nodded.

"There's a phone call for you. It's one of your advertisers."

"I'll pick it up in my office," Helena said. She turned to the girls. "Excuse me, I need to take this call. Then I'd better hand over the original of that kidnap note to the police detectives. Then I'm going home." She sighed. "It's been a long day. Thank you all for coming down here. You can't imagine how much I appreciate your help."

She reached into the pocket of her jacket, pulled out a business card, and wrote something on it. "This is my home phone number," Helena said. "Please don't hesitate to call me at home if you need to."

"We'll be in touch," Nancy said, taking the card.

"Will you be talking to the police?" Helena asked.

"Yes," Nancy said. "I'm particularly interested in whether any fingerprints turn up other than the station employees'. I'll check with Chief McGinnis about it later."

Nancy turned to her friends after Helena was gone. "I'd say we already have two suspects."

"Right," George said. "First, there's Neal Graham, who actually seemed glad to have Dan out of the way. And second, Ray Ludlow, who gets rid of his competition with Dan off the air."

"What about Lenny Gribble?" Nancy asked.

"What?" both Bess and George said in surprise. "You think he's a suspect?" Bess asked in disbelief.

"That skinny kid?" George asked.

"Well, Lenny may say he's Dan's Biggest Fan, but he's also a brand-new deejay at KRCK who wants to be on the air," Nancy replied.

Just then, down the hall, the door to the announcer's booth swung open, and Lenny ran out. He looked up and saw the girls in the lobby at the end of the hallway.

He grinned and said, "Gotta get a drink of water before this song is over." Then he held up his fist in a "thumbs-up" sign. "Can you believe it? I'm finally ON THE AIR! I think I'll call myself the 'Lean, Mean Man'!" Then he whooped and took off down the hall.

Bess and George stared at Nancy.

Nancy nodded. "See what I mean?" she said. "Lenny Gribble has a perfect motive for wanting Dan Wildman out of the way—ambition. And that makes him a prime suspect!"

4

In Dan's Apartment

"I think I'd better have a talk with Lenny," Nancy said to her friends. "I'll stick around until he's off the air. You two can wait if you'd like or catch a bus home."

"I think I'll wait," Bess said. "This is going to be an interesting case. Radio celebrities and kidnapping and everything!"

"I'll wait, too," George agreed. She looked at her watch. "It's getting close to nine o'clock. Ray Ludlow should be showing up pretty soon."

"Right," Nancy said, nodding. "I want to talk to him, too."

The girls decided to wait in the radio station lobby, out of the way of the police. The police officers had gone, but the detectives were still there, taking statements from station employees.

Nancy spotted the gray-haired detective who had questioned her when she, Bess, and George had first arrived at the station. He had eyed the girls with interest and a fair amount of suspicion several times since they passed him in the hall. Nancy wondered if he had called Chief McGinnis yet to check her out.

The girls had just seated themselves on a large couch in the lobby when the front doors burst open and a well-built man with light brown hair and dark eyes stalked into the station.

"What in blazes is going on here?" he asked anyone within earshot. "What's this 'emergency' I heard about from my answering service?"

The girls looked at one another excitedly. They all recognized the deep, smooth voice of Ray Ludlow.

Nancy jumped up and approached him. "Excuse me, Mr. Ludlow," she said. "My name is Nancy Drew, and I've been asked by Helena Santos to help with the investigation—"

Ray stared at Nancy. "The investigation of what?"

Nancy studied his face a moment. He certainly seemed surprised. Or maybe he's just a good actor, she thought.

She continued to watch him carefully as she

told him. "I'm sorry, Mr. Ludlow, but Dan Wildman has been kidnapped."

"*What?*" Ray looked genuinely shocked.

"Yes, he was on the air, doing his show. Someone came in and overpowered him. He was only able to yell for help before he—"

Ray Ludlow burst out laughing.

His outburst startled Nancy. "What's so funny?"

"You fans are all the same," Ludlow said, gulping with laughter.

Nancy stared at him. "What do you mean?"

"You'll believe anything," Ludlow said, grinning. "Like the time Dan told listeners that Martians had landed on a farm outside River Heights." The deejay shook his head. "That guy doesn't know that KRCK is a rock station. He thinks it's a comedy station."

"Well, this is no joke," Nancy said. "See those men over there?" She pointed to the two police detectives. "They're detectives from the River Heights police force. Dan Wildman really has been kidnapped, Mr. Ludlow. My name is Nancy Drew, and I've been asked to help with the investigation."

Ray Ludlow looked over at the two police detectives, then back at Nancy. "So, it's the real thing," he said. "Well, what do you know about that."

"Finally, he gets the message," George murmured to Bess.

Just then Neal Graham appeared in the lobby.

"Good, you're here," he said, seeing Ray. "We've been trying to reach you."

"I went for a drive," Ray said. Nancy thought he sounded defensive, and she wondered why.

Graham obviously thought so, too. "Hey, that's okay," he said. "I don't expect you to stand by just in case one of the other deejays gets into trouble. And that Wildman's more trouble than he's worth. Get down to the announcer's booth now. I'll want you to take over Dan's show, or at least part of it. But I might have to let that kid Gribble get some air time. Audiences like variety."

"Audiences like *me*, you know that, Neal," Ray said with a grin, as he disappeared down the hall with Neal Graham close behind him.

Bess turned to her friends.

"Can you believe that guy?" she said. "And he seems so nice on the air. He didn't seem to care at all about what happened to Dan Wildman. He's just interested in himself!"

"He thought Dan was pulling one of his tricks," George said. "At first, anyway."

"He doesn't seem too unhappy that Dan has been kidnapped, that's for sure," Nancy said thoughtfully. "It means he's getting more air-

35

time." Nancy paused for a moment, then she said, "You know, if Ray Ludlow were the kidnapper, he could keep Dan out of the way just long enough to make Dan's popularity plunge and *his* ratings go up. Then he'd let Dan go. When Dan eventually showed up no one would believe his story. Everyone would still think it was a hoax. After all, Dan has done a lot of crazy things before."

"And maybe Dan would be fired for being a troublemaker!" George said.

"Exactly."

"I think you might be on to something, Nancy," George said with obvious admiration.

Just then, Lenny, having been relieved by Ray Ludlow, scurried down the hall and into the lobby.

"Did you hear me on the air?" he asked, grinning. "How'd I sound? Great, right?" Lenny had a loud voice. He seemed to naturally talk about ten decibels above everyone else.

"No, they didn't pipe the broadcast into the lobby," Nancy said.

Lenny continued to grin. "I was really up for this, you know? I've been getting ready for my first broadcast for years! What a lucky break!"

Then he realized what he'd said, and his face turned a deep red.

"Oh, I mean, it's really horrible about Dan,"

he said, and his voice got louder as he became increasingly nervous. "I just hope that something really awful hasn't happened to him. I mean, being kidnapped is awful, but I hope he's okay. It'd just be too terrible for the world to lose that guy, that great deejay, I mean, the world would be a much lesser place, you know, if he—if something really serious happened to him. I really care about the guy. In fact, I was hoping you'd let me help you with your investigation— I'd do anything for Dan—really, I *am* his biggest fan. I use Dan as my model for the kind of deejay I'd like to be. I mean, I have my own style and everything, but I think he's the *best,* don't you?"

He stopped, blinking, and looked from Nancy to Bess to George and back again.

The girls stared at him, speechless.

"I mean—" he started to say.

"We know what you mean," Bess said quickly, to stop him from making another speech. "But I don't think we really need more help—"

"Oh, but I can get you into Dan's apartment," he interrupted.

The girls looked at one another, then back at him.

"We'd love your help," Nancy said sweetly. "When can you take us?"

He grinned. "How about now?"

* * *

A full moon was rising when Nancy and the others headed toward the car. The KRCK building and trees cast long shadows into the street.

"So how did you get Dan's key?" Bess asked Lenny, as they all piled into the car.

"I've been a gofer for Dan since I started working at the studio," he said.

"What do you do?"

"I 'go fer' coffee, 'go fer' something he forgot at home. Just general errands. But he let me follow him around the station, and I learned a lot watching him while he was on the air." He grinned. "If you'd listened to my broadcast, you'd have seen what I mean." He shook his head. "That guy was so *good!*"

"*Is* so good," Bess corrected. "He'll be back." She looked at Nancy and smiled. "Nancy will find him."

Lenny's cheeks grew pink again, and he nodded. "Sure, he'll be back. I can't wait to see him again."

Lenny directed Nancy across town. They arrived at an apartment complex sprawled across a large grassy lawn. Huge oak trees shaded the four timber-and-glass buildings which made up the complex. In the center of the complex was a swimming pool, which sparkled under the bright lights surrounding it.

Nancy pulled into a parking area next to the second building.

"This is a nice place," Bess said. "Have you been here a lot?"

"Just to run some errands for Dan," Lenny said.

The girls got out of the car and followed Lenny down the sidewalk and into the building. Just inside the heavy wooden front door was a flight of stairs which Lenny headed up, taking two at a time.

"I love this place," Lenny said, a big grin on his face. "As soon as I'm on the air regularly and can afford it, I want to move in here, too."

At the top of the stairs, Lenny turned left and headed down the hall. Nancy hoped he wasn't going to talk in his normal loud voice before they got into the apartment. She didn't exactly want to advertise to the other tenants that they were walking into Dan's apartment.

But she didn't need to worry. Lenny didn't say a word until he stopped in front of number 12. He pulled the key from his pocket, slid it into the lock, and opened the door.

"After you, ladies," he said, and made a sweeping gesture with his arm toward the open room.

"Dan's bedroom is just down the hall," Lenny said, pointing at a hallway to their left. "And his study is just across from it. Feel free to look around."

Nancy headed into Dan's study first, hoping to find a clue to his whereabouts.

"What exactly are we looking for?" Lenny's voice called out loudly as he followed her down the hall.

"Anything that might give us a clue as to why Dan was kidnapped," Nancy said. "Maybe Dan wrote a note to himself or maybe there's a letter from someone who is angry with him. It's hard to say. I just hope that if there *is* a clue, we'll recognize it."

"Oh, we'll find *lots* of letters to him," Lenny said. "He's always getting fan letters, especially from junior and senior high school girls." He grinned. "But they won't be angry letters." He laughed loudly. "Far from it!"

Nancy sighed and wished Lenny would talk a little less frequently and a lot more quietly. He was pretty irritating to have around.

One thing she had to admit to herself, though. Lenny didn't seem like a guy who was harboring a dark criminal secret. He seemed too open, too bumbling, too—well—*silly* to be a kidnapper. Unless he was acting.

"Oh, man! Look at *this* letter!" Lenny exclaimed.

"What? What?" Bess and George came running from the bedroom. "Did you find a clue?"

40

"'Dan the Wild Man,'" he read, "'I think you are the funniest, cutest guy on the air!' There's an exclamation point after that," Lenny said, grinning. He continued. "'I would *love* to meet you. I just know we'd get along *very well,* if you know what I mean!!' *Two* exclamation points!" Lenny shook his head and laughed. "This is great, this is great! Isn't that a great letter?"

Bess rolled her eyes.

"Lenny," Nancy said sharply, "we appreciate your help, but we're looking for *clues* here, not for prospective dates for Dan. Get it?"

Lenny gulped. "Oh, sure. Sorry."

Nancy sighed and went back to work. Lenny was right about one thing. Dan didn't seem to have any enemies, if the stack of letters on his desk was any indication. While several criticized his crazy antics on the air, none of them sounded particularly angry. And most of the letters were similar to the one Lenny had read aloud.

Besides the letters, there were dozens of autographed eight-by-ten glossy photos of himself that he was obviously preparing to send out in answer to his fan mail.

Dan was indeed a popular guy.

The rest of the apartment offered nothing in the way of a clue. After a half hour more of searching, Nancy had to admit that they weren't going to find evidence that would finger anyone in the kidnapping.

"What now, Nancy?" Bess asked.

"I wish I could tell you," Nancy said, frustrated.

"Well, I still work at the station," Lenny said. "I could be a spy, and like, keep my nose to the ground, so to speak, and maybe I'd overhear something that might help you."

"I don't think so," Nancy said. "But thanks for offering." She didn't want to break the news to him that he wasn't exactly spy material.

"Didn't Helena Santos say that she was going to hire an intern in the production office?" George asked suddenly.

"That's right," Lenny said. "It's a temporary part-time position."

"That's right. She mentioned that she was going to put an ad in the paper," Nancy said. She looked meaningfully at George.

"I can't," George said. "Remember, I have to help my cousin get ready for her wedding next week."

"How about you, Bess?" Nancy asked. "I'd do it, but too many people in River Heights know I'm a detective, and after the kidnapping, they'd know for sure why I was there. If someone at the station is responsible for the kidnapping, they'd have their guard up if I were there."

Bess made a face. "Something tells me I'm going to be trying out *all* those typewriters I saw in nearly every room of the station."

Nancy nodded seriously. "We do need to see if any of them matches the lettering of the ransom note."

"But there are hundreds of them!" Bess wailed.

Lenny spoke up. "Oh, no, Bess. I'm sure there couldn't be more than fifteen or twenty, counting the old ones in the store room." He turned to leave the room. "You know, I'm thirsty. I don't think Dan will mind if I steal one of his sodas." He disappeared in the direction of the kitchen.

Nancy turned to Bess. "Will you do it?" she asked her friend.

Bess groaned. "Twenty typewriters. Give me a break!"

"It would really be a big help, Bess," Nancy said.

"Okay, okay," Bess said, pulling herself up. "I'll do it for you, Nancy, and Dan Wildman."

"Thanks, Bess," Nancy said, grateful for her friend's help. "I'll call Helena when I get home to set it up."

Bess smiled. There was a faraway look in her eyes. "Dan will probably want to thank me in person," she said dreamily.

"We have to find him first," George reminded her cousin.

"The sooner, the better," Nancy said in a serious tone. "After looking at these letters and seeing how incredibly popular Dan is, I'm worried about his safety. Ray Ludlow—if he *is* the kidnapper—might not let Dan go. He may want him out of the way—permanently."

5

Talking to Neal Graham

Helena Santos had agreed to hire Bess as a production intern, so at eight o'clock the next morning, Nancy drove her friend to KRCK for her first day of work. Already in the parking lot were vans from three television stations and two newspapers in the area. Several people were unloading video equipment from a station wagon parked at the far end of the lot.

"Uh-oh," Nancy said. "This case is really going to get a lot of publicity."

Lenny arrived as Bess was getting out of the car. He walked over to Nancy's car, leaned in the passenger's side window, and grinned at Nancy.

"Look at all the media coverage we're getting!" Lenny declared loudly. He was obviously impressed. "Maybe we'll be on TV, Nance."

Bess rolled her eyes. "Lenny, nobody calls her *Nance*."

"Okay, sorry," he said, still smiling, and straightened up. "Ready to go to work, Bess? We'll *fight* our way through the crowds of reporters and get to the head of the line. Get it? Headline?" He laughed hilariously at his own joke.

"I get it, Lenny," Bess said with a sigh. Then she leaned down to smile at Nancy. "I'll keep my ears and eyes open for anything that might help."

"Great," Nancy said. "And, Bess, thanks a lot."

Lenny's head popped into the window again. "I'll take good care of her, Nancy, don't you worry about that."

Bess cleared her throat. "Great, Lenny, thanks," she said, with an obvious lack of enthusiasm. Nancy tried not to smile.

Lenny certainly was trying to be helpful. Maybe he's trying a little *too* hard, Nancy thought. But that just might be his style. Unless his style is a deliberate cover-up, to hide the fact that *he's* the kidnapper.

Nancy sighed as she watched them walk into the building. She felt frustrated about this case, and at the moment, she really didn't know where to go for more information. Helena had already told her all she knew about the station and the employees who might be involved in the kidnapping. Lenny certainly seemed eager to help, but even if he wasn't the kidnapper, it didn't seem likely that he was going to provide any key information that would help her solve this case.

The other players in the mystery, Neal Graham, Tom Cottner, and Ray Ludlow, weren't at all interested in talking. At least, they hadn't been last night.

Nancy decided it was time to talk to Neal Graham about the rivalry between Ray and Dan. The station owner certainly had not been friendly last evening, but perhaps he had cooled down a bit since then. It was worth a try.

She parked her car and entered the building. The lobby was filled with reporters. They came in all shapes and sizes and both genders. Some held video cameras or lighting equipment, others were hauling out microphones and notepads. Nancy made her way to the reception desk.

A tiny brunette woman sat behind the desk. She looked bewildered in the middle of all the hubbub. The nameplate sitting next to a small green plant in front of her said Angela Fenley. She forced a smile when Nancy approached.

"Hi," Nancy said. "I'm Nancy Drew. Would it be possible for me to see Mr. Graham?"

The woman looked doubtful. "Do you have an appointment, Ms. Drew?" she asked.

"No, I don't," Nancy said. "But I'm helping with the kidnapping investigation, and it would be very helpful if I could talk with him."

"I see," she said, and smiled faintly. "Just a moment, please." She lifted the telephone receiver to her ear and pushed three buttons. "Nancy Drew is here to see you," she said. "Shall I send her back?"

The smile faded as she listened to her employer and she nodded silently. "Okay," she said. "Yes, Mr. Graham, I'll tell her." She hung up.

"I'm sorry, Ms. Drew," the woman said, "but Mr. Graham says to tell you that he won't talk to you and that the police are handling the case."

Nancy nodded. She wasn't surprised. Nevertheless, she felt very disappointed.

"I see," she said thoughtfully. "Well, thank you for trying, Angela." Then she had an idea. "By the way, is Helena Santos here yet?"

"Sure, she's in her office," Angela said. "She came in about twenty minutes ago." She picked up the phone again. This time after announcing that Nancy was here, she looked up smiling. "Ms. Santos says to come right on down."

"Thanks again," Nancy said. "Uh, Helena's office is near Mr. Graham's, isn't it? I can never remember."

"Yes, just one door past his," Angela said.

48

"Oh, right," Nancy said with an innocent smile.

Of course, Nancy already knew where Helena's office was; she'd been there last evening. But now she knew where Neal Graham's office was, and that's where she headed now.

She didn't bother to knock, just opened the door and walked in.

Neal Graham was on the telephone. He looked up, astonished, when Nancy entered.

"That's all I know at the moment," Neal Graham said, eyeing Nancy angrily. "Yes, I'll give you an interview as soon as we know anything."

He hung up the phone and opened his mouth to speak.

Nancy held up a hand. "Mr. Graham," Nancy said before he could say a word, "don't blame Angela. She passed along your message that you didn't want to talk to me. She thinks I came back here to see Helena."

Graham stood behind his desk. "Of all the insolent—" His face grew red with anger as Nancy had seen it yesterday. "I told you to keep your nose out of my business, and I meant it!" He shook his head. "I've got a hundred people who all want to talk to me. And they will give the station publicity that might, just might, give the station a boost in advertising sales. So tell me, for the love of Mike, why should I talk to *you!*" He stopped and glared at Nancy. "I shouldn't have

fired my security guard the day before yesterday.
If I had hired a new one, believe me, I'd have him
throw you out!"

If you'd hired a new one, you wouldn't need
my help or the help of the police, Nancy thought
to herself. A security guard might have stopped
the kidnapper.

"All I need is a minute of your time," she said
aloud. "Helena told me how concerned you are
about this station and Dan Wildman. I'm sure you
want Dan to be found before anything terrible
happens to him."

"Well, of course I do," Graham said. "I want to
get this nightmare over with. I've got enough
other things to deal with—I don't need a kidnapping, too."

Nancy started to speak. "Mr. Graham—"

"I'll give you a minute," Graham said gruffly,
"and then you will go. Understand?"

Nancy nodded and smiled. "Of course. Thank
you, Mr. Graham."

Neal Graham sat again behind his desk. "So,
get on with it."

"Tell me about the rivalry between Dan
Wildman and Ray Ludlow," Nancy said, seating
herself across the desk from him.

Nancy had intentionally acted as if it was
understood that there *was* a rivalry, so that
Graham wouldn't dismiss the idea.

"Well, what do you expect?" snapped Graham.

50

"Ray's spent years practicing and perfecting his style. He's climbed to the top of his profession. So you can't blame him for being a little protective of his turf."

Nancy leaned forward. "Does Ray feel threatened by Dan?"

Neal Graham shifted uneasily in his chair. "Well, yes, I guess you could say that," he said. "Dan was a young guy coming in here. In a short time, he really shook up the place."

"He was drawing fans away from Ray's show?" Nancy asked.

"Our research shows that more people are listening to Dan now," Graham conceded. "That means Ray and Dan are competing with each other for listeners. I think that kind of competition is healthy."

Nancy's eyes widened. "You do?"

"Sure," he said. "It keeps these wise guys on their toes. They have to work harder. A deejay who's worried about keeping his job is not a lazy deejay."

"I thought you and Ray Ludlow were good friends," Nancy said.

"We are," Graham said. "But my station comes first, before anything." He gazed evenly at Nancy. "Including friendship."

"I see," Nancy said.

Neal Graham stood up. "Look, I hope you don't think Ray Ludlow had anything to do with

51

the kidnapping of Dan Wildman," he said. "Ray is a solid citizen. A good, loyal employee. You'd be wasting your time if you give any more thought to suspecting Ray in this case." He rounded his desk and strode to the door. "And now, let's not waste any more of *my* time."

Nancy rose. "Thank you, Mr. Graham. I appreciate your talking to me."

"Did I have a choice?"

Nancy cleared her throat. "Yes, well, thank you anyway." She nodded goodbye and left. She heard Graham close the door behind her.

Nancy glanced down the hallway and saw Helena peeking out of her office. The woman smiled and gestured to her to come in.

Nancy stepped into Helena's office and closed the door.

"How did it go?" Helena asked. "I heard him yelling, so I looked in on you. I thought you might need my help. But then he seemed to calm down a little, so I came back here."

"Well, Mr. Graham was pretty polite, considering that I barged into his office after he asked me to leave the building," Nancy replied.

Helena smiled. "I knew he'd come around, Nancy. He really isn't such an awful person. Oh, that reminds me, you might want to listen to the radio later on this morning."

"Why?"

"Neal Graham has ordered round-the-clock appeals on the radio for information about the kidnapping. His spots start airing this morning at eleven o'clock."

"I guess you're right about Graham," Nancy said. "Maybe he really *does* care about Dan."

"Not only that, he's offering a fifteen-thousand-dollar reward to anyone who comes forward with information that leads to the arrest and conviction of the kidnappers."

"Fantastic!"

"His bark really is worse than his bite," Helena said.

"Helena, I hate to say this, but . . ."

"But what?"

"Could Neal Graham's concern possibly be motivated by the publicity that the kidnapping is bringing him? He said that the station might be getting more advertising money because of Dan's kidnapping."

Helena considered what Nancy had said. "Well, I wouldn't be at all surprised if the kidnapping brings in more advertising clients for the station. Local business owners know that large numbers of people will be listening to KRCK to find out what happened to Dan Wildman. Did you see all the media people out there in the lobby? This story will be all over the news tonight. People will tune in to our station and business owners know that. They'll buy air time on the station for their commercials." She sighed. "That's what pays the bills, Nancy, and keeps the station running."

Nancy nodded. "I understand," she said.

"I guess the prospect of large advertising revenues could prod Neal Graham into offering a generous award. That would certainly bring in more listeners."

Nancy nodded again. "Thanks, Helena, for being so honest."

"I don't think Neal had anything to do with the kidnapping, though," Helena said. Nancy noticed a note of uncertainty in her voice. Helena studied Nancy's face. "Do you?"

Nancy kept her tone neutral. "I just don't know," she said. "We'll have to see what develops." It had occurred to Nancy that Neal Graham just might have engineered the kidnapping to bring in more advertisers—and more money. But she didn't want to share her new theory with Helena yet. Helena was a loyal employee of Neal Graham, and Nancy didn't want to risk losing the station manager's support in this case.

Nancy said goodbye and stepped into the hall. Bess, with Lenny close behind, was walking toward her.

Bess shifted the files she was carrying and waved a greeting. "Did you see all the reporters out in the lobby, Nancy? Isn't that something? They were there when we arrived and they're still waiting for something to break on the case."

"So am I," Nancy said.

"They interviewed me!" Lenny said. "You know, for going on the air right after the kidnapping with the tribute to Dan!" Lenny sounded proud of himself.

"By the way," Bess added, "Helena gave me a bunch of jobs to do, like errands and filing. But she knows I'll be on the lookout for clues, too."

Nancy nodded. "That's great, Bess. Which reminds me. I know you're not looking forward to it, but I really think that the next step in this case is to check those typewriters," Nancy said. "If we find that the ransom note was written on a station typewriter, we'll know for sure that someone here was responsible for the kidnapping."

Bess sighed. "Okay," she said. "I'll get on it during my break."

"I'll help you," Lenny said. "We'll work on it together."

There was a slight pause. "Okay, thanks," Bess agreed. "The work will go faster that way."

Nancy thanked them both and left the station. She drove directly to the police station and found Chief McGinnis in his office hunched over some paperwork that was spread out on the desk in front of him.

"Good morning, Chief," Nancy said. "I've just been at KRCK. There's a huge mob of reporters hanging out there."

The chief shifted in his chair and gestured for Nancy to sit down.

"Yes," he said. "I heard that Helena Santos, the station manager, asked you to help with the investigation."

Nancy grinned. "One of your detectives was pretty suspicious of me at first."

The chief dismissed it with a wave of his hand. "Marsden was just doing his job," he said.

"I know," Nancy said. "Actually, I came by to ask you what you'd found out about the fingerprints. I saw several of your people dusting for prints just after the kidnapping last night."

The chief leaned back in his chair. "They matched the station employees who are in and out of the announcer's booth every day."

Nancy counted them off on her fingers. "That means Dan, Ray, Neal Graham, Lenny, and Helena."

Chief McGinnis nodded. "Right, and a few other deejays at the station who barely know Dan. And of course, Jim Flagg."

Nancy was startled. She thought she was familiar with all the station employees.

"Jim Flagg? I haven't heard the name. Who's he?"

"The station janitor," McGinnis said. He leaned forward and looked Nancy directly in the eyes. "You also might be interested to know that Jim Flagg is the only one of that group who does *not* have an alibi."

6

A New Suspect

It was lunchtime when Nancy left Chief Mc-Ginnis's office. When she got into her car, she flipped on the radio. KRCK was broadcasting its appeal for information on the kidnapping of Dan Wildman. "I hope it works," Nancy murmured to herself.

Nancy decided to stop back at the radio station to see if Bess had any news for her. But first, she'd have a talk with Helena Santos about Jim Flagg.

She caught up with Helena as the station manager was heading out the door of her office.

"Got a minute?" Nancy asked.

Helena smiled. "For you, yes. Those media people have finally left, so I thought I'd dash out for some lunch. But I'd be glad to talk to you. I'll have the coffee shop on the corner deliver a sandwich." She gestured toward two chairs in a corner of her office.

"This will only take a few minutes," Nancy said, seating herself. "Tell me about Jim Flagg."

Helena joined Nancy. "Our janitor?"

"Yes."

Helena thought a moment. "Well, he's been here forever. I've been here fifteen years and he'd been here a while before that."

"What's he like?"

Helena shrugged. "He's a nice man. He's pleasant with everyone at the station. He really just goes about his business and doesn't bother anyone." She chuckled. "He kind of blends into the surroundings, I guess."

Nancy nodded. "Did he get along with Dan Wildman?"

"Sure," she said. "As I said, Jim gets along with everyone."

"Hmmm." Nancy was stumped. The chief had said he was the only suspect without an alibi the night of the kidnapping. "Can you think of any reason why Jim Flagg could possibly be involved in Dan's kidnapping?"

Helena rose thoughtfully from her chair and moved to her desk, her back to Nancy. "Well . . ."

"Helena, the most important thing right now is to get Dan Wildman back. In one piece."

Helena sighed. "Yes, I know. It's just that . . ." She turned to face Nancy. "Well, Jim has had some troubles lately, and I don't want to add to them. Nancy, he couldn't possibly be involved! If you met him—"

"I will meet him, Helena," Nancy broke in. "But I need you to tell me everything you know about him."

Helena turned and faced Nancy. "Okay, I suppose that when the police check on him, they'll find it out anyway."

"Find out what?"

"Well, he's been in to see Neal Graham frequently the past several weeks to ask—maybe *beg* is the right word—to beg for a raise and for more time off."

"Why?"

"Jim's wife is very ill. She's been in the hospital for a month now. She had a serious and very expensive operation. Jim is desperate to get money to pay her medical bills. But he also wants time off so that he can be with her." Helena shook her head sadly. "I think the poor man's going to pieces. I feel so sorry for him."

Nancy sighed. "That would be hard for anybody. He must be miserable." She leaned forward in her chair and spoke gently. "But, Helena, I've got to consider all the possibilities here. If Jim Flagg is desperate for money, as you say, he would have a pretty good motive for kidnapping Dan and making a ransom demand. Especially if he didn't get that raise he'd been hoping for. He might feel that the station owed it to him."

Helena frowned. "Well, that's true, but it's still hard for me to believe that Jim would resort to kidnapping someone to get what he wants."

"Think of it this way—what is most important to him?" Nancy asked.

"His wife," Helena said. "Yes, I get your point."

"I think I should talk to him, Helena," Nancy said softly.

"I agree," Helena said. "But I'll be honest with you, I don't know where he is right now. I haven't seen him lately."

"Okay," Nancy said. She stood up. "I'll catch him later. Thanks for telling me about Mr. Flagg, Helena."

Helena smiled and said goodbye.

Nancy found Bess and Lenny in an office down the hall. Bess was sitting behind a typewriter, typing out a copy of the kidnap note, checking the typeface against the photocopy of the original.

"How's it coming?" Nancy asked, entering the office and plopping down in a soft chair near the door.

"Nothing yet," Bess said, studying the paper

under the paper roll. "Nothing even very similar. And this makes the tenth typewriter we've checked."

"Well, keep working on it," Nancy said. "We certainly could use a break in this case."

"It could be anyone, *anyone* at all!" Lenny said dramatically. Even when he was dramatic, he was loud, Nancy noticed. He stood up and began pacing around the office. "Ray's got a motive, Mr. Graham's got a motive—"

"You've got a motive," Bess said.

Lenny stopped abruptly and stared at Bess. "What?"

"Sure," Bess said. "Who got a chance to work on the air for the first time yesterday?"

Lenny went pale. "You don't really suspect *me*, do you?" He looked from Nancy to Bess and back to Nancy again. "You do? You think that *I* had something to do with Dan's kidnapping?"

Then something surprising happened. A slow smile spread across Lenny's face. "Ye-e-a-h," he said. "I suppose I *could* have pulled that off. To get myself on the air and start my career!"

Bess rolled her eyes. "Oh, give me a break!"

Lenny laughed. "Talk about a publicity stunt! I'd be famous—I'd be a household name—"

"You'd be an inmate in the state pen," Bess finished his sentence for him.

Nancy smiled. "Well, we have to look at every

possibility, but let's just say that you're not the number one suspect, Lenny."

"But I *could* have done it," Lenny said proudly, a big grin on his face. "I bet I could've gotten away with it, too!"

Bess shot a desperate look at Nancy. "What are we going to do with this guy?"

Nancy laughed and said only half-kidding, "Keep an eye on him."

Just then, anxious voices came from down in the lobby.

"I thought the media people had gone," Nancy said. They hurried down the hall toward the commotion.

"What's going on?" Bess said.

The reporters in the lobby had all circled Angela Fenley's desk and were hurling questions at her. She was close to tears.

Bess and Lenny disappeared into the crowd while Nancy elbowed her way to the front. "Angela!" she called above the other voices. "What is it? What's happened?"

Angela shrugged, bewildered. "They say there's a new development in the kidnapping. Why am I the last to know?"

She picked up her telephone and pushed three buttons. "Ms. Santos?" Angela nearly shouted into the receiver. "You'd better come out here!"

Nancy turned to find Bess and Lenny. Bess had

disappeared, but Lenny was poring over a newspaper at the edge of the crowd.

Just then, Helena Santos arrived, holding a sheet of typing paper. The men and women rushed toward her, turning on their lights, sticking microphones into her face, and shouting questions at her.

"When did you get the message?"

"What time did you hear from the kidnappers? Exactly what were their words?"

"Is the station prepared to pay all that money?"

"What does Neal Graham say? Does he think that Dan Wildman is still alive?"

Helena held her hand up for quiet.

"I have a statement here from Neal Graham, the owner of KRCK," she said. She held the paper up and read, " 'We at KRCK are very concerned about the welfare of employee Dan Wildman and are hoping for his safe return. Beyond that, I have no statement to make to the press at this time. You must understand that this man's life may be in danger. The police have requested, for his sake, that we not talk about the case. My offer, however, of fifteen thousand dollars still stands for anyone who comes forward to the police with information that leads to the arrest of the kidnappers. Thank you.' "

Immediately, the reporters began shouting questions at her again, but Helena shook her

head no and said, "I have nothing more to say."
She turned and walked back down the hall.

The reporters, some of them muttering in disappointment, moved back into the lobby. Nancy caught sight of Lenny as he casually approached another of the reporters. He began talking to her, his hands thrust in his pockets. Within a minute, he was surrounded by other reporters. The television lights were switched on and microphones were thrust in his face.

"What's he doing?" Nancy looked up to see Bess standing next to her.

"I don't know, but we'd better find out," Nancy said. "I hope he isn't going to talk too much."

They moved closer and pressed up as close to Lenny as they could get.

"Yes, I'm helping with the investigation," he was saying. "We've narrowed down the list of suspects a bit—"

"Oh great!" Nancy said. "Bess, I've got to stop him before he messes up our investigation."

"What are you going to do?" Bess asked.

Nancy thought quickly and smiled. "Just watch!"

Bess watched Nancy move around the crowd and approach Lenny from behind. Nancy tapped him firmly on the shoulder and whispered something in his ear. Lenny looked surprised and excited. "Really?" he said to Nancy.

Lenny turned again to the reporters surrounding him. "That's all for now. I'll talk to you again when we have new developments."

Nancy, with her hands firmly on Lenny's shoulders, guided him directly out the front wooden door and down the sidewalk. Bess hurried out after them.

Lenny turned around. "Hey, what's the idea? Why are we outside? I thought you said the network people were on the phone asking for me."

"Keep walking, Lenny," Nancy said between her teeth. "Don't stop till you get to my car. And for heaven's sake, keep your voice down, will you?"

Nancy opened her car door and shoved Lenny inside. Bess crawled in and shut the door.

"Hey, what gives?" Lenny asked loudly.

"Lenny! What were you doing in there?" Nancy asked angrily. "You had no business talking to the press that way!"

Lenny frowned. "I wasn't telling them anything they didn't already know!" he said defensively.

"What do you mean?" Nancy asked. "What, exactly, *do* they know?"

Lenny held out the newspapers he'd been carrying since Helena made her statement to the press.

"What?" Nancy asked. She took the paper and

read the headline, "KRCK Receives Ransom Demand." She skimmed the article and handed it to Bess.

"What is it?" Bess asked.

"Someone contacted this paper," Nancy said. "The caller identified himself as one of the kidnappers. He said that he and his partners have contacted the radio station. They want half a million dollars, or Dan the Wild Man is dead!"

7

Searching for Clues

Bess skimmed the paper in front of her.

"It says here that the ransom demand was made anonymously over the phone at six A.M. to KRCK," Bess said. Then she began to read from the top story. " 'Police were tracing phone calls that came to the station. When the ransom demand came in, it was instantly locked in with the communication center at the police station.' " She continued to read. " 'Several squad cars were sent immediately to the location of the calls, a phone booth at Spoon Drive and Fortieth, but the caller had disappeared.' "

Bess read on silently, then looked up. "The caller phoned several newspapers from different phone booths and told them all about what he'd told KRCK."

Nancy nodded. "It sounds as if the kidnapper was afraid that the media might not hear about it unless he clued them in." She opened the car door. "Come on. Let's go back and ask Helena why she didn't tell me about the ransom demand."

They piled out of Nancy's car and headed back into the station.

They found Helena in her office.

"Yes, the station did receive the ransom demand," she admitted. She smiled apologetically at Nancy. "I'm sorry I didn't tell you, Nancy. Neal Graham absolutely forbade me to say anything to anyone about it. But now that the newspapers know . . ."

"But I thought he *wanted* the publicity for the station—to get advertising dollars," Nancy said.

Helena shrugged. "That's just Neal Graham's style. He runs hot and cold, constantly changing."

"He could have made those calls himself," Nancy said thoughtfully.

"You mean to the newspapers?" Bess asked.

"Right," Nancy said. "He'd certainly know that calling in the newspapers would create a lot more publicity for the station."

"Oh, Nancy, I can't imagine that Neal could be

involved in Dan's kidnapping," Helena said. "I know you have to consider everyone a suspect, but Neal Graham just wouldn't do that."

Nancy wondered why Helena was so sure that Neal Graham wasn't involved in the kidnapping. Was she covering up for him? Or was she just a completely loyal employee?

Aloud, she said, "If we could just find the typewriter that typed the ransom note. Then we'd know we weren't completely wasting our time looking for the kidnapper at the station."

"Sorry, Nancy," Bess said. She looked over at Lenny. "It's been a dead end so far, but we'll keep at it."

Nancy looked at her watch.

"Helena, will you give me Ray Ludlow's address? And can Bess take a lunch break? I'd like her to come with me for a while. If you can let her go for an hour," she added quickly.

Helena smiled. "Go ahead, Bess. I think we'll manage. I'll see you back here later this afternoon." She wrote down Ray Ludlow's address on a piece of paper and handed it to Nancy.

Nancy and Bess left the station and headed out to Nancy's car.

"Where are we going?" Bess asked. "In the near vicinity of food, I hope. I'm starved!"

"If we have time, we'll stop for a bite," Nancy said.

"Only a bite?"

Nancy laughed. "Okay, a whole, entire lunch. But I'd like to talk to Ray Ludlow first." She looked at her watch. "What time was George supposed to be home from shopping? Wasn't she going to help her cousin choose the flowers for her wedding?"

"Right," Bess said. "I think she said she'd be available after one."

"It's one now," Nancy said. "Let's pick her up on the way to Ray Ludlow's apartment."

George was home and ready to help with the investigation.

"I'll bet we looked at two hundred pictures of floral arrangements!" she said, groaning. She climbed into the backseat of Nancy's sports car. "What a way to spend a morning! I'm ready to think about something more exciting than miniature roses and baby's breath!"

"We may have one lead in this case," Nancy told the girls as she pulled away from the Faynes' house.

"What?" both girls said at once.

"Chief McGinnis says there's one person whose fingerprints were found in the announcer's booth who doesn't have an alibi," Nancy said.

"Well, let's hear it," George said. "Who?"

"His name is Jim Flagg," Nancy said. "He's the janitor at KRCK."

"Oh, Lenny told me about him," Bess said. "His wife is very sick, and he needs money badly

71

for her medical bills. But really, Nancy, he doesn't sound like a criminal type. Lenny told me that Ray Ludlow lost a very expensive gold watch last month. He took it off because the band was pinching his wrist. He forgot it at the station, but the next day, Jim Flagg came into his office and gave it to him. He'd found it and wanted to return it." Bess leaned back in the passenger seat and folded her arms. "That doesn't sound like a criminal to me."

"I suppose," Nancy said thoughtfully, "that someone could have hired Flagg to kidnap Dan. He might have agreed to do it because he's so worried about his wife."

"But that brings us back to square one," Bess pointed out. "Who would hire Jim Flagg to do something like that?"

"How about Ray Ludlow?" George said.

"Or that awful Neal Graham?" Bess added. "*Everybody* seems to dislike that man."

"Except Helena Santos," Nancy said.

"This is really way out in left field," George said, "but do you think Helena Santos set up the kidnapping to help the station and her boss, Neal Graham?"

"She was the one who asked for our help," Nancy pointed out. "But that would be a good way to divert suspicion from herself. I'd hate to think that she could be responsible for the kidnapping, but at this point, we can't rule her out as a suspect. Especially since she didn't tell me about the ransom demand." Nancy sighed. "We really can't accuse anybody until all the evidence is in. The problem is, that's just what we *don't* have—evidence." She shook her head. "This case is totally baffling."

Twenty minutes later, Nancy pulled into the parking lot of Ray Ludlow's two-level, redbrick apartment building. Like the complex that Dan Wildman lived in, this building was attractive and well cared for, with a swimming pool for its tenants in the back.

They located his apartment number on the mailboxes just inside the front door and climbed the stairs to the second floor. Stopping in front of #27, Nancy knocked firmly on the door. She waited a full minute and knocked again.

"Probably out taking care of his kidnap victim," George said jokingly.

"I still think Neal Graham is the guy we should be investigating," Bess whispered.

"Shh," Nancy warned. "Probably most of the tenants are at work, but just in case, we have to be quiet."

She reached into her pocket and pulled out a credit card.

"Nancy!" Bess said. "You're going to break in?"

"I'm going to *let* myself in," she said. "I'll leave everything exactly as I find it. I just want to have a

73

look around. Keep an eye out for me. Bess, stay here. George, stand at the top of the stairs. Let Bess know if anyone's coming."

She slid her card in between the door and the doorjamb, flicked her wrist, and gently eased the door open. Then she slipped into Ray's apartment and closed the door gently behind her.

The drapes were drawn at the living room window, and the apartment was in deep shadows. Nancy didn't dare to open the drapes or turn on a light; someone might see it from outside and come up to investigate. She reached into her purse and pulled out her small flashlight. Aiming the light so that the beam didn't hit the window, she made a quick check of the five small rooms: living room, kitchen, bath, and two bedrooms. Nothing out of the ordinary caught her eye.

She was looking in the second bedroom when she spotted something on the top of the bookshelf. An old typewriter.

Could it be the machine that typed the kidnap note?

Nancy dragged a straight-backed wooden chair over to the shelf and climbed onto it. She managed to pull the machine down from the shelf without losing her balance. It was difficult; the typewriter was large and heavy and very awkward to lift from below.

Hugging the typewriter to her body, she lowered herself from the chair to the floor, then carried it to a desk next to the window, and carefully set it down.

She found a piece of scrap paper in the wastebasket and rolled it into the typewriter.

Just then, she heard Bess's muffled whisper at the door. "Nancy, he's coming! Ray's coming! Get out! *Hurry!*"

Nancy looked around desperately for a place to stash the typewriter. If Ray found it on the desk, he'd know immediately that someone had been there. It was much too heavy to lift back up on the bookshelf in the next few seconds. Nancy quickly set it down on the floor on the far side of the desk so that it was hidden by the bed and couldn't be seen from the doorway.

She heard a rattle at the apartment door. Ray was coming and it was too late to escape!

8

Confronting Ray

Nancy dove behind the bed and lay still.

She heard the door close and footsteps tread softly on the carpet across the living room. A drawer was opened and closed and then the footsteps were in the hallway. Then Nancy heard the sound of running water.

Nancy lay on the floor, her heart pounding. She hoped that Ray would close himself in the bathroom, to give her time to escape.

But the running water stopped and the footsteps came closer. He seemed to be making stops in each room and then going to the next.

Then she remembered. She hadn't locked the door behind her when she'd entered the apartment! Ray must have tried his key and found the door unlocked.

Ray knew someone was in the apartment! That's why he was stopping in each room, why he was so quiet.

He was looking for her!

What should she do? There was no way for her to escape without him seeing her. Nancy's first impulse was to slide all the way under the bed. But if he were looking for someone who was hiding, he would definitely look there, too. She decided to stay where she was.

Suddenly the room was flooded with light. Then a hand reached over the bed, grabbed hold of her arm, and hauled her to her feet. Nancy cried out in pain.

"Okay, what are you doing here?" Ray Ludlow demanded. He released Nancy's arm and looked at her angrily. "You're that amateur detective, Nancy Drew. I should have you arrested for breaking into my apartment. That'll teach you not to go snooping around."

Nancy took a deep breath. She knew she had to stay calm. She faced Ray and looked him squarely in the face.

"I'm just doing my job, Mr. Ludlow," Nancy said coolly. "If you'd been the least bit helpful with this investigation you might not have become a suspect."

Nancy knew she was taking a big chance confronting Ray Ludlow. He might become violent. She hoped George and Bess were within shouting distance if anything happened.

But Ray just stood there and looked at her, his mouth opened in surprise. *"I'm* a suspect!"

Nancy eyed him levelly. "That's right," she said. "Everyone knows that you don't like Dan Wildman, that you're threatened by his popularity. You might even be worried about losing your number one spot at KRCK. No one could reach you just after Dan was kidnapped . . ."

"I was taking a drive!" Ray interrupted angrily.

"And," Nancy added with emphasis, "you don't seem to care about what is happening to Dan. He was overpowered and dragged away from the station where you work, and you don't seem at all upset about it."

"Why should I be upset?" Ray said, folding his arms and leaning against the desk. "While Dan is gone, his listeners will tune in to *my* program. They always used to," he added bitterly.

"Are you saying you're glad that Dan was kidnapped?" Nancy asked in disbelief.

"Of course, I'm glad!" Ray said. "Besides, I'm sure he'll be all right. It's not as if he's in great danger."

"And how would you know that?" Nancy asked pointedly.

"Because," Ray said, "it's obvious who kidnapped him."

"Care to fill me in?"

Ray's mouth twisted in a wry smile. "I thought you were supposed to be the great detective." When Nancy didn't respond, he continued. "Okay, I'll tell you," Ray said. "The person who is most desperate for money. Isn't that the classic motive for kidnapping someone and asking for ransom? It's our custodian, Jim Flagg. His wife is very ill, you know."

"Yes, I know," Nancy said.

"That's why I'm not worried about Wildman," Ray said. "Flagg may need money badly, but he's not a killer. He just needs the money. As soon as he gets it, he'll let Dan go, and Dan will run back to KRCK and live happily ever after."

"Will *you?*" Nancy asked. "That is, if your scenario works out the way you've just described it?"

Ray shrugged. "Maybe I'll keep some of the Wild Man's listeners. I've been working on some ideas to liven up my show."

"I see," Nancy said.

"That's what I was coming back home to work on," Ray said. "Which brings me to the subject we were on a moment ago. Breaking and entering, I believe, is the legal phrase we're looking for. But then, you should know that."

"I'm not as sure as you are who the kidnapper is," Nancy said.

"And you think *I* am the kidnapper?"

"Well, you do have a good reason for wanting Dan off the air."

Ray smiled contemptuously and tipped his head back a little, watching Nancy through nearly closed eyes. "Prove it."

"Maybe I can," Nancy said.

"How?"

Nancy leaned down, grabbed hold of the typewriter, and hefted it up on the desk. The scrap paper she had inserted earlier was still in the roll. From the pocket of her jeans, she took out a folded piece of paper.

"This is a photocopy of the kidnapper's note," Nancy said. "Do you see the *n*'s, the way they slant just slightly to the right?"

Ray examined the paper. "Yeah, so what?"

Nancy seated herself at the desk and typed the kidnap message. Then she rolled the scrap paper out of the typewriter and held it up next to the photocopy.

Nancy gazed up at Ray. "A perfect match, letter for letter. Even the slanted *n*'s."

Ray laughed.

Nancy placed the note she'd just typed over the original. She could see through the scrap paper she'd typed on, and the message lay over the original perfectly.

Ray laughed again.

"Pretty smooth, Nancy Drew," he said. "You proved that the kidnapper's note was typed on this typewriter, all right. There's only one problem, though. That typewriter doesn't belong to me. It belongs to KRCK. I checked it out last night and brought it home to do some work."

"Can you prove that?"

"Of course I can! I signed it out. The date and the machine's serial number are written on the sign-out sheet at the station. Check it out."

"I will," Nancy said.

"Anyone at the station could have used that typewriter," Ray said. "Including Jim Flagg."

"Okay," Nancy admitted. "Maybe you're right."

"I know I'm right!" Ray said nastily. "And now that I'm off your suspect list, would you mind getting out of here."

"I'm going," Nancy said. "And I'm sorry about breaking in here. I haven't had much to go on, and I really wanted to help Helena Santos. And Dan Wildman."

Ray grunted and turned away.

Nancy left quietly and found Bess and George in a panic down the hall.

"What happened?" Bess asked. "Oh, Nancy, we were so worried!"

George checked her watch. "In two more minutes we were going to call the police."

"Thanks, you two," Nancy said. "But I'm okay."

She filled her friends in about what happened and told them about finding the typewriter they'd been looking for. She explained that Ray had checked it out from the station. But she made a mental note to check the sign-out sheet at the station.

"So we're back to square one again," Bess wailed.

"Well, at least we know that someone at the station was responsible," Nancy said. "And we know it's likely that Ray Ludlow's not the kidnapper. So, we haven't been completely wasting our time."

She drove George home.

"How about a late lunch?" Nancy said, pulling away from the Faynes' house. "I'll call Helena from whatever restaurant we decide to go to and tell her you'll be a bit later than we thought."

Bess's mouth dropped open. "I can't believe it," she said. "I haven't thought about food since you sneaked into Ray Ludlow's apartment. How about that! I forgot about eating, I was so worried about you!"

Nancy smiled. "Well, I appreciate your concern, Bess."

"But don't think you have to risk your neck every time I need to take off a few pounds."

They laughed.

"How about the Hungry Fork?" Nancy asked. "The food is good and the service is fast."

"Great!"

Nancy pulled the car into the parking lot at the restaurant and the girls went inside.

"I love this place," Bess said. "All these plants!"

Wooden beams near the ceiling were lined with English ivy and philodendron that trailed over the rims of their pots and hung down over the lunch crowd. A fig tree grew in a large container in the middle of the small restaurant, and each table was decorated with a small plant.

They ordered chicken sandwiches, French onion soup, and lemonade. Then Nancy left to call Helena.

"Thanks for working at the station," Nancy said, when she had returned from making the phone call. "It could really help us solve this case. Just have to keep your eyes and ears open. You may hear things that you don't think have anything to do with the case, but they might be important clues."

Bess sighed. "Well, I don't mind the job, really. I'm learning a lot about how a radio station is run. I didn't know that the deejay business was so competitive! Did you know that KRCK receives demo tapes from deejays at smaller markets all around the country who want to come and work there?"

"Demo tapes? Markets?" Nancy laughed. "You're catching on to the radio business fast, Bess."

"Anyway, demo tapes are audition tapes on cassette," Bess continued. "These deejays work at stations that reach smaller numbers of people—so their advertising doesn't reach as many people. That's what a 'smaller market' is all about. Deejays want to work in larger markets in big cities where there are more listeners."

Nancy nodded. "I get it."

"And the deejays at KRCK make demo tapes to send to even bigger markets so they can move onward and upward," Bess said. "One of my jobs is to open the packages containing these tapes and write down in a notebook who they're from and file them with the others." She sighed. "That part of it is pretty boring, actually. I'll be glad when we get this case wrapped up."

Nancy smiled. "So will I."

"So what's your next move, Nancy?"

"Everyone I talk to gives me information that seems to point to Jim Flagg," she said, "and he doesn't have an alibi for the night of the kidnapping. I'm going back to the station after lunch to talk to him."

"Do you think he's the kidnapper?" Bess asked.

"I don't know," Nancy said. "But if he doesn't want to become our number-one suspect, he'd better come up with a strong alibi!"

9

A Silent Suspect

It took Nancy nearly half an hour to find Jim Flagg. Nobody seemed to know where he was. Finally she asked Lenny if he'd seen the janitor.

"Yeah, I saw him heading down to the basement about a half hour ago. Are you going to question him?" he asked anxiously. "Do you think he's the kidnapper?"

Nancy didn't answer his questions. Instead she thanked him and hurried to the stairs near the front door.

At the bottom of the steps, she saw Jim Flagg. He was a short, heavyset man dressed in gray work clothes and heavy work shoes. He was standing over a large table, working on the electrical cord of a large blue lamp.

"Jim Flagg?" she said.

He turned toward her and gave her a friendly smile. "Yes?" he said. "What can I do for you?"

Nancy hesitated. Flagg had glistening blue eyes set in a little round face. A pair of wire-rimmed glasses sat on his upturned nose. Nancy thought that if he put on a white beard and a red suit, he'd make a perfect Santa Claus.

"My name is Nancy Drew," she said. "I'd like to ask you a few questions if you don't mind."

"Sure," he said. "What do you want to know?"

This wasn't going to be easy. Nancy didn't want to upset Flagg, but there were questions she needed to ask him. It was the only way she'd be able to eliminate him from her list of suspects. "Helena Santos asked me to investigate the kidnapping of Dan Wildman," she said.

"Yes," he said. "A shame. Dan's a real nice guy."

"Yes, he is," Nancy said. "We're all anxious to get him back safely. So I'm talking to everyone at the station who might have been close by when it happened. I'm trying to piece all of the information together."

"I don't know if I can be of any help," Flagg said. "I've been pretty distracted lately."

"I know," Nancy said sympathetically. "I understand your wife is ill."

Flagg sighed deeply. "She's in pretty bad shape," he mumbled. "I worry about her a lot."

"I understand," Nancy said gently.

"I don't know what I'd do without her," he said, "and everything's so expensive these days." He shook his head sadly. "The medical insurance doesn't even cover half of the cost. I'm about wiped out, I guess, what with doctor bills, hospital bills, medicine . . ."

"I'm sorry," Nancy said.

"She could get better care if I were a rich man." A note of bitterness crept into his voice. "I keep thinking she'd have done better marrying someone else." Flagg looked at Nancy. "She could've married anybody she wanted to, you know. My Mandy was a beautiful woman. Beautiful. Still is, too." His voice trailed off and a faraway look came into his eyes.

"Mr. Flagg," Nancy said softly, "I'm sorry that I have to bother you with these questions right now. I know that your mind is with your wife."

Flagg nodded. "The doc wants to give her a new medicine. Try it out, you know. He thinks it might help her." Flagg looked at the floor. "But it's so expensive, I—I can't pay for it."

"I'm sorry, Mr. Flagg. It must be terribly difficult for you."

Nancy let a few seconds pass before she spoke again.

"I'm sorry, Mr. Flagg, but I need to ask you a few questions."

Flagg sighed deeply again. "Sure. Go ahead."

"I need to know where everyone was the night of the kidnapping. Can you remember what you were doing?"

Flagg stood silent; he turned his face away from Nancy.

"Mr. Flagg?"

Still, he didn't answer. Nancy let a full minute go by.

"Mr. Flagg, I need to know," Nancy said. "I need you to tell me where you were."

"I don't want to talk about this anymore," he said. His voice became hard. "I have a lot of work to do here, Ms. Drew. I'd like you to leave me now so that I can do it."

"But—"

"Please, Ms. Drew, I'm not trying to make trouble. I just don't want to talk about it. I already told the police as much."

Nancy thought a moment. There must be a way to get Flagg to talk. Why was he being so difficult? He couldn't possibly be the kidnapper, she thought. Or was she letting her heart make that decision instead of her head?

The truth was, she didn't *want* to believe that Jim Flagg was guilty.

"All right," Nancy said slowly. "I guess there's nothing I can do to force you to talk to me."

She turned and walked to the bottom of the stairs. Then she turned back to Flagg. "But I hope you'll change your mind." Flagg didn't respond. "If you do, please call me." She took a pencil and notepad from her purse, wrote down her phone number, tore off the sheet of paper, and handed it to him.

Flagg took the piece of paper and nodded stiffly but didn't speak.

Nancy climbed the stairs to the main floor and headed for the lobby.

"Any luck?" Bess asked. She had just walked down the hallway and into the lobby.

"Mr. Flagg doesn't want to talk," Nancy said.

"He wouldn't tell you where he was during the time Dan was kidnapped?" Bess frowned. "Does he know that he's the main suspect?"

"I don't think that would matter to him," Nancy said. "Something's going on here that I just don't understand." She shook her head. "It's just like working on a jigsaw puzzle. But I can't make the puzzle fit together because too many important pieces are missing."

She stood there, biting her lip thoughtfully.

"Uh-oh," said Bess. "I can see the wheels turning. You're thinking up a plan, right?"

Nancy looked at her friend. "Bess," she said, "do you think that we could get everyone together here? Including Neal Graham?"

"I don't know," Bess said. "You could ask him. What do you have in mind?"

"A replaying of events that took place on the

night of the kidnapping. We'll talk through it," Nancy said. "Maybe some of the missing pieces will fall into place." She turned toward the hallway. "I'll ask Neal Graham right now."

Nancy was a little surprised that Neal Graham went along so easily with her idea.

"I'll do anything at this point," Graham said. "This thing is driving me crazy."

Within five minutes all of the major players were together. Nancy looked around the lobby. Helena sat with Lenny on the couch; Ray Ludlow and Tom Cottner sat on overstuffed chairs in the corner. Neal Graham stood, his arms folded, waiting to begin. Bess dragged in a metal folding chair from one of the offices and sat down.

"Jim Flagg can't be here," Helena told Nancy. "It's his break, and he's spending it over at the hospital."

Nancy nodded. She was disappointed that he wasn't there, but she understood his need to be with his wife.

"Okay," Nancy said. "We're going to go back over everything that happened the night of the kidnapping. I'm sure that most of you have re-played in your minds what you were doing that evening. Now we're going to talk it through. This may or may not work. What I'm hoping for here is that one of you will remember something—even if it seemed totally insignificant at the time—

anything that might help us pinpoint who was involved in kidnapping Dan Wildman. Are you all ready?"

Neal Graham found a chair and sat down.

"You bet!" Lenny spoke up. "This is just like something you'd see in a detective show on TV."

"I think we're all ready to find out what went on that night, Nancy," Helena said.

"Okay," Nancy said. "Now, everyone think of where you were that night. Try to visualize the jobs you were doing. Close your eyes if that helps you to concentrate."

"Well, if you remember correctly, Ms. Drew," Ray said with a hint of sarcasm, "I wasn't even *at* the station that evening."

"Yes, we all know that," Lenny said, rising from his chair. "You *said* you were out driving your car somewhere."

Ray stood up and took steps toward Lenny. "I don't like the tone of your voice, Gribble. Just what are you implying?" Ray said, his voice rising in volume, nearly matching Lenny's.

Lenny put his hands up playfully in front of his face as if to ward off any blows from Ray.

"Just kidding, Ray," he said, grinning, as he hopped away. "Don't hurt me!"

"Come on," Helena said in an exasperated tone. "Let's do this for Nancy. Maybe something will turn up."

Everyone settled down, and each person

closed his or her eyes to try to remember what they were doing that night. Nancy let them sit in silence for a few moments.

"Okay, Helena," Nancy said finally. "You go first. Tell us what you were doing."

"I was clearing some papers off Neal Graham's desk," she said, her eyes still closed. "I filed some of them, put several books back on the shelf above his desk, and threw away some scratch pads Neal had been doodling on."

"Did you hear anything unusual as you cleaned?"

Helena frowned. "No—I don't think so. I don't remember anything."

"Were you listening to Dan's show while you worked?" Nancy asked.

"No, I usually do, but I didn't listen to it that evening. Sometimes we even pipe it into the lobby, but not always."

"Was it piped into the lobby that night?"

"No," Helena said. "I'm sure of that. I would've heard it from Neal's office if it had been. I'd left the door open."

"Okay, good," Nancy said. "Tom?"

The engineer rubbed his forehead, his eyes closed. He smiled sheepishly, but when he spoke, his tone sounded defensive. "I was in the lounge at that time of the evening," he said.

"Taking a break?" Nancy asked.

"Dan said I could go grab a cigarette."

93

"Did you ask him if you could leave?" Nancy asked.

"No, he just suggested that I might like a break," Tom said.

"Was it your usual break time?"

"No. But Dan had been doing that for the last, oh, week or two. I guess I'd asked him once not too long ago if I could go for a cigarette. So from then on, he just offered to let me go during a slow time."

"Better kick that habit," Lenny said. "Those cigarettes'll kill you."

Tom scowled. "Yeah, thanks for the health tip, Gribble."

"Tom, did you hear anything out of the ordinary?" Nancy asked.

"Nope."

"See anything unusual?"

"Hey, I was in the lounge," he said. "There are no windows to the outside or to the hall. And because of the cigarette smoke, the door is always kept closed. It's like being in a tomb, especially with the hum of the soda and snack machines."

"Okay," Nancy said. "Lenny?"

"*Well*," he said loudly, smiling, now that he was center stage, "I'd run an errand for Dan to the soft ice cream store—he'd been eating chocolate sundaes nearly every night for the past week or so—and I'd just gotten back. Dan asked me to go to the station library to pick up some carts that he wanted."

"So, he sent you out, too," Nancy said.

"Did you get the carts?"

"Sure! I did anything Dan wanted," Lenny said. "But I'd forgotten my key, so I went back to get it. Hey! I'd forgotten that part. Yeah, I went back to get the key from Dan's desk."

"Did you have to go past the announcer's booth to get to the library?"

"Sure," Lenny said. "It's right on the way."

Nancy leaned forward. "Did you see anyone suspicious in there?" she asked.

Suddenly, Lenny sat bolt upright, his eyes still closed. "Yeah, I did!"

Lenny's eyes flew open and he stared at Nancy, a look of astonishment on his face. "I saw Jim Flagg! *He was in the announcer's booth!*"

10

A Fiery Situation

"So that's why Jim Flagg refused to talk to you about an alibi, Nancy," Bess piped up. "He didn't *have* one!"

Helena sighed deeply and stood up. "I guess I'd better go and call the police," she said. She turned to her boss. "Oh, Neal, I hate to do this."

Graham's stern face didn't change. "I know, but it certainly looks as if Flagg is the person we're looking for." He shook his head. "I knew Flagg needed money, but I had no idea how desperate he'd become."

Helena disappeared down the hall to her office.

Lenny approached Nancy, his eyes big as saucers. "Boy, I really blew this case wide open, didn't I?"

Nancy nodded, her face grim. "You certainly did, Lenny."

"Boy," he said, shaking his head, "that little piece of information is going to put Flagg away forever. Just because I saw him in the announcer's booth when I did. Whew!"

"What now, Nancy?" Bess asked.

"I think I'd better go and talk to Jim Flagg before the police get here," Nancy said. She shook her head. "I still can't believe he's the only one who kidnapped Dan Wildman. If only he'd talk to me!"

Once again, Nancy headed down the stairs to the basement. After a little searching, she came to a small, dimly lit room filled with cleaning products, a large metal bucket on wheels, mops, a floor polisher, and a vacuum cleaner. The lamp that Jim had been working on earlier was sitting on a small table in the corner just inside. The only light came from the lamp on the table.

Jim Flagg was carefully hanging some tools on a pegboard on the wall.

"Mr. Flagg?" Nancy asked.

Flagg turned around, and when he saw who had called his name, his body sagged a little as if a heavy weight had been added to his shoulders.

"I thought we were finished talking," he said. His voice was dull and sad.

"Mr. Flagg, you have to talk to me now," Nancy said.

"I have something to do upstairs now," Flagg said. "I'll be right back."

He abruptly left the little room, closing the door behind him. As the door latched shut, Nancy heard it click loudly. She walked up to the door and tried the knob. The door wouldn't open.

"Mr. Flagg!" Nancy called out. "You locked the door!" Nancy waited a moment, then she called out again, "Mr. Flagg!" There was no answer. The janitor had apparently gone upstairs.

Then Nancy remembered the lamp. She studied it and saw that it had a three-way bulb. She'd turn it up and then see if there was some way she could unlock the door. Nancy wondered if he'd locked her in on purpose. And if so, why.

She stepped over to the lamp on the table and looked for the switch. She found it and flicked it up another notch.

Instantly the lightbulb flashed, making a short buzzing sound.

The lamp cord! Flagg had been working on it. It must have a short.

With a *ffffftt*, a rag sitting on the table under the lamp exploded into flames and ignited other rags and newspapers nearby.

Nancy took off her jeans jacket to extinguish the fire, but the flames only grew in size.

Coughing on smoke, Nancy ran to the door and tried to push it open. She rattled the knob. She looked for a key or latch on the inside to open the lock, but there was none.

There was no way out!

"Help! Help!" Nancy yelled, as she banged on the door with her fists.

But it was no use. The people upstairs were too far away to hear her cries.

The fire was burning brighter. The table under the lamp was now engulfed in flames.

Nancy ran to the shelves and gathered up all of the cleaning solvents. These products were flammable and would explode, sending the entire room up in one big ball of fire.

Her throat was dry and burning and her eyes were beginning to sting. The smoke was getting so thick she could barely see. She stumbled to the farthest corner of the room and set her armload of cans and bottles on the floor. Standing up, she steadied herself with one hand on the back wall.

Suddenly her hand slid over a wooden frame at the side of another large pegboard that hung on the wall.

It felt like a window frame! Nancy pushed her hand behind the board and felt the smooth surface behind it.

It *was* a window, and it had been covered over with black paint!

Nancy blinked back the tears from her burning

eyes and quickly ran her hands over the peg-board. The board was fastened only at the top. Grabbing a screwdriver and hammer from the pegboard, she quickly turned the screw at one corner, pushed the board aside, and squeezed around it.

She shielded her face and thrust the hammer through the window.

Cool air rushed in through the broken window, and Nancy gulped in great lungfuls of it.

It was very hot in the little room, and the flames were growing, getting nearer. With a last effort, she finished hammering out the glass and pulled herself through the basement window to safety.

Nancy dragged herself out of the window and onto the grass. She was coughing hard, and it took a full minute before she could breathe normally. She took in several big breaths of fresh air, then forced herself to her feet and staggered around the side of the building. She could hear sirens in the distance.

The parking lot was in her view now, and she spotted Jim Flagg ducking into an old Chevrolet.

"Stop!" Nancy yelled, hoping that someone was nearby and would see him. "Quick, stop him! He's getting away!"

11

An Arrest Is Made

Just then, a fire truck pulled into the lot, followed by a police car. Someone called them, thought Nancy. Just in time.

Two men got out of the police car. Nancy called to them, pointing to the Chevrolet. "That's Jim Flagg! He's getting away!"

The tall, gray-haired detective Nancy had spoken to just after the kidnapping waved his hand, and a uniformed police officer ran to stop the janitor.

Detective Marsden stood on the sidewalk and watched Nancy make her way toward him.

"What happened to you?" Marsden asked, staring at her in disbelief. Nancy was aware that she was covered from head to toe with a thin film of black soot from the smoke, and that her eyes were red and still tearing. She coughed several times.

Marsden took her arm and led her toward the police car. "I think you'd better sit down," he said. "Don't talk until you've caught your breath."

Nancy sank gratefully into the seat on the driver's side of the car.

"What happened to you?" Marsden repeated.

Nancy coughed again and ran a hand through her tousled hair. "I was talking to Jim Flagg in the basement. He locked me inside a small room."

"And he set fire to the place?" the detective asked.

"No, I did that," Nancy said. "By accident. But he may have set me up. He left a dimly lit and defective three-way lamp there and locked me inside. He must have known that I'd try to turn up the lamp to get more light."

"What lamp?"

"He was working on a lamp earlier," Nancy said. "It had a short in it—it was dangerous. When he left, I tried to turn up the lamp and it threw sparks all over and they caught fire." She thought a moment. "And then he ran away."

"He seems guilty to me. Sounds like we've got our man, all right," the detective said.

* * *

"I just can't believe that sweet man is a criminal!" Bess said.

Bess, Lenny, and Nancy were discussing the case over coffee at Cherie's Cafe, a block from the station. They'd stayed with most of the other employees until the firefighters had extinguished the blaze in the basement. Fortunately, because the door had been closed in the small room, the fire had been contained inside. Lenny expressed horror at the danger Nancy had been in.

"I'm sure glad you found the painted-over window," he said.

"Not as glad as *I* am!" Nancy said. She laughed, but she was still a bit shaky from her ordeal in the little storage room.

"And Jim locked you inside?" Lenny asked. "I just can't believe it. Everyone's known Jim for years. First, he's a kidnapper and now this!"

Bess sighed now and sipped her coffee. "It's hard to imagine. Doesn't he look like a sweet old grandfather?"

"Or Santa Claus?" Nancy said.

"Oh, you can never tell who's guilty just by looking at them or being around them a short time," Lenny said. "You know, the most unlikely suspect is always the one who commits the crime."

"Had a lot of experience with criminals, have you, Lenny?" Bess asked, irritated.

He shrugged. "Well, I watch a lot of television and read a lot of books," he said.

Nancy smiled. "Well, I understand what Bess is saying. Flagg certainly doesn't fit the criminal stereotype."

"But he ran away!" Lenny said loudly, grinding his finger into the table. "That proves his guilt!"

"Well, it doesn't actually prove it, but it certainly makes him look very suspicious," Nancy said. "We'll have a hard time proving his innocence now."

"Why would you want to?" Lenny cried. "The man locked you in a burning room and almost killed you!"

"It wasn't burning when he locked the door," Nancy reminded him.

Then she looked him straight in the eye. "But I'll answer your question. I want to prove his innocence because, like Bess, I still can't believe that he's involved in Dan Wildman's kidnapping."

"What did Flagg say to the police when they arrested him?" Bess asked.

"He wouldn't say anything," Nancy said. "When they asked him where he'd been going in such a hurry, he refused to speak to them. He won't say anything to defend himself! That's what's so odd. Most criminals will try to defend themselves at least."

"Well," Lenny said, "maybe all of this just shows he's inexperienced with crime."

"What do you mean?" Bess asked.

"Well, maybe he was so desperate for money, kidnapping Dan Wildman was the only thing he could think of. It was a crazy idea, but maybe he decided to do it because he doesn't know how to rob a bank."

Bess thought about that and sighed. "Well, maybe you're right."

Nancy nodded. "I hate to admit it, Lenny, but maybe for once, you *are* right."

That evening, Nancy sat at the dinner table with her father and Hannah Gruen.

Worry lines creased Hannah's face. "Nancy, you've hardly touched your food. Are you worried about the case you're working on?"

Nancy, her elbow on the edge of the table, had been pushing the food around on her plate with a fork. She put down her fork, leaned her chin in her hand, and looked wearily at Hannah and her father sitting across the table from her.

"I'm sorry, Hannah. I know this meal took half the afternoon to fix, and it's very good. It's just that I've been working so hard to find the kidnapper. And the more I investigate, the more answers I get that I don't like. And questions I can't answer."

"You look tired," Hannah said.

"I'm more frustrated than tired," Nancy said. "But I guess I'm kind of tired, too."

"What's happening with the case?" Carson Drew, Nancy's father, asked.

"Well, I've uncovered some evidence and all of it seems to point to one person, but I just can't believe that he's guilty. He seems to be such a nice man."

Carson Drew had stopped eating while Nancy was talking. Now he put down his fork. "Nancy, the guilty person isn't always the one you suspect."

Nancy smiled wryly. "Lenny told me that— loudly—just a little while ago."

She paused and leaned over the table toward her father. "Dad, in your law practice, have you ever had a client who you had a lot of faith in, whom you believed with all your heart to be innocent, but who turned out to be guilty?"

"Rarely," Mr. Drew said. "It isn't easy to accept, but it does happen. Sometimes, Nancy, people do things in times of desperation that they would never do under normal conditions."

"Maybe that's what happened in this case," Nancy said. "Mr. Flagg's wife is seriously ill and he needs money for her care."

"I can't think of a more extreme circumstance," Mr. Drew said. "People do amazing things for their loved ones. Sometimes pretty crazy things when all else fails."

Nancy shook her head slowly. "I don't know, Dad. That description does fit Jim Flagg, but somehow I can't believe he's guilty."

Nancy left the rest of her food untouched. It had been a very long day. She left the table and trudged upstairs to bed.

Nancy tossed and turned all night. She kept dreaming and waking with thoughts of Jim Flagg sitting in jail while his wife lay ill in the hospital.

When dawn came, she was wide awake. She decided to get up and plan her strategy for the day. She still hoped that something would turn up to clear Jim Flagg of the charges that had been brought against him.

Maybe it would help to talk to him one more time, Nancy thought. Spending the night in jail might have changed his mind about talking to her.

It was too early to leave for the station when she finished dressing, so she turned on the early morning news. Jim Flagg's arrest, as well as the fire at KRCK, were the top stories.

Nancy shut off the TV before the news reporters began their in-depth accounts of what happened. She couldn't bear to hear about Jim Flagg.

She made some toast and ate it while she paced back and forth over the kitchen floor. It was a good thing Hannah wasn't up yet, Nancy thought. She would have worried that Nancy hadn't gotten enough sleep and hadn't eaten enough breakfast.

Nancy was ready to leave and heading for the door when the telephone rang. She raced to it so it wouldn't ring a second time and wake up her father and Hannah.

"Hello?" she said.

"Nancy!"

She held the receiver away from her ear as Lenny's voice blasted through the phone.

"Lenny, what is it?" Nancy asked. "You sound upset."

"Nancy!" Lenny sounded out of breath, huffing with excitement.

"Lenny, calm down," Nancy said. "What's going on?"

"It's the case . . . the case . . ."

"What, Lenny? What's happened? Where are you?"

"At the station. I got here early."

"Okay," Nancy said. "What happened at the station?"

"Never mind," Lenny said. "You've got to get here quick!"

"Why? What is it?"

"We're—You're going to have to start another

investigation," he said breathlessly. "You're going to have to start all over again!"

"What!"

"It was here this morning when I arrived!" he said. "It was right on my desk!"

"What *was* it?" Nancy asked, trying to get a calm response out of Lenny.

"It proves that they've arrested the wrong man!"

"What do you mean?"

"The police arrested the wrong man! I have proof right here! Jim Flagg didn't kidnap Dan Wildman!"

12

Double Messages

Nancy wondered what proof Lenny had that would clear Jim Flagg. But by now, she'd had enough experience with him to realize that Lenny dramatized events. Most likely, whatever he'd discovered could wait a few extra minutes.

Nancy really wanted to see Jim Flagg after his night in jail. Maybe he would answer her questions now and help himself.

When she got down to the police station, she was allowed to see Flagg, but as the officer on duty warned, "only for a few minutes."

She was shown into a small room. Moments later, Flagg was brought into the room. He sat across a little table from her. He rubbed his hands together nervously and fidgeted in his chair.

"Jim," Nancy said, "I wish I could make you understand how important it is for you to talk to me—or someone else who can help you."

"*I'm* not the one who needs help," he said, and stood up. He began to pace back and forth in the small room like a caged animal. "It's my wife."

"You *both* need help," Nancy said. "Please, Jim, you can't help her if you're locked up in jail."

"She needs me!" Jim said.

"Of course she does," Nancy said, watching him pace.

Jim stopped abruptly and slammed his fist into his palm. "I may not be able to provide for her the way I wish I could. But I *can* cheer her up!" He stared at the wall. "I could always make her laugh, no matter how down she'd get."

"Jim—"

Jim turned to Nancy. His eyes were pleading. "I have to get out of here," he said. "I have to be near her. She'll never make it if I can't keep her spirits up."

Nancy sighed deeply. "I know how important it is that you be with her. And I'm doing everything I can to help you do that, believe me. But please, you've got to tell me where you were that evening when Dan Wildman was kidnapped."

111

Jim Flagg turned his back on Nancy. "I have nothing to say." She barely heard him mumble. "Nothing."

Nancy left him, her heart aching, and headed for the radio station.

Please let this lead of Lenny's be a good one!

Lenny ran out to meet Nancy when she pulled into the parking lot.

"What took you so long?" he yelled. "I've been here for hours! I came early this morning because I couldn't sleep."

"I couldn't sleep either. I stopped at the jail," Nancy said. She followed Lenny up the sidewalk to the front door.

"Hardly anyone's here yet," Lenny said. He waved his arms in the air, excited. "You won't believe this! What terrific luck!"

"What?" Nancy said. "What *is* it?"

"When I got here this morning," Lenny said, leading Nancy through the lobby and down the hall, "I found a cassette tape waiting for me. At first, I just assumed that it was another audition tape from some hopeful deejay looking for a job."

"Don't they usually come through the mail?" Nancy asked.

"Yeah, right, but this one wasn't in an envelope," Lenny said. "I found the tape on my desk in the production office. It definitely wasn't there yesterday."

Nancy nodded. They walked into the office.

112

"I wanted to start working, to get my mind off everything else for a while," Lenny said.

"Lenny, is this story leading up to something?" Nancy asked impatiently.

Lenny didn't answer. Instead, he moved to the desk and picked up a cassette.

"I got curious, so I listened to it." He held it up in front of Nancy's face. *"This,"* he said dramatically, "is going to free Jim Flagg!"

Just then, Neal Graham passed by the door on his way to his office.

"Mr. Graham!" Lenny yelled, and hurled himself out the door. "Wait! You'll want to hear this, too!"

Graham looked as tired as Nancy felt. Maybe he hadn't gotten any sleep last night, either, thought Nancy.

"What is it?" Graham asked.

"Come in here. I'll play it for you both." Lenny led the way to a small room at the end of the hall and pushed the door open. The tiny room was filled with electronic equipment.

"We record a lot of commercials in here," Lenny explained to Nancy.

There was barely enough room for the three of them. Nancy watched as Lenny pushed the cassette into the large machine which stood on the floor and was taller than Neal Graham. The equipment could accommodate both cassettes and reel-to-reel tapes. Lenny pushed a button.

113

In a moment, a voice spoke. "Hello, this is Dan Wildman."

"What!" Neal Graham said. "Where did this tape come from!"

"It was left on my desk in the production office," Lenny said.

"I know that you're worried about me," Dan said, "and I want you to know that I'm okay. I'm being treated well." Even though his voice was shaky, Nancy thought he sounded okay.

"But I've been told that it is *imperative* that you get the ransom money together. When you have it ready, broadcast the announcement over the air. You will then be contacted with instructions about what to do next." There was a pause. Then he said, "I can't say any more now. Please hurry. My life depends on it." Then silence.

Lenny looked up at Nancy. "Do you feel better about Jim Flagg now?"

Nancy nodded. "I see what you mean. This tape was delivered while Jim Flagg was in jail. So he couldn't be the kidnapper."

Graham spoke up. "Not necessarily. Flagg could be working for someone else. With Flagg in jail and not able to help, maybe his partner in this crime decided to continue on his own. In fact, the kidnapper may even have liked the idea because he wouldn't have to share the ransom money."

Nancy thought a moment. "I wish Dan had given us a clue about how many kidnappers there are," Nancy said. "Did you notice? He didn't say whether he was being held by one person or more."

"Maybe he was reading something the kidnappers had written for him," Graham said.

"Probably," Nancy agreed.

"Well, I'm going to have to pay the ransom," Graham said. "Wildman said his life depends on it. We can't gamble with his life."

"How are you going to get the money?" Lenny blurted out. Nancy frowned meaningfully at Lenny but he didn't seem to notice.

"I don't know," Graham said. "Five hundred thousand dollars is a huge amount of money. I've been making some calls, but I haven't been able to raise it."

Nancy studied the station owner. If he was that determined to raise the ransom money, maybe it meant that he really did care about Dan's safety. On the other hand, maybe Flagg was working for *him*, and his concern was just a big cover-up.

Nancy felt a wave of frustration wash over her. If I could only find the clue or clues that would solve this case once and for all, she thought.

"Lenny," she said, "tell me everything again about this tape."

"What do you want to know?"

"Are you *positive* that it didn't come in the mail yesterday? Maybe you didn't see it there on the desk."

Lenny shook his head. "Bess and I already listened to the tapes that arrived yesterday. And we filed them all away."

"I'm sure that there won't be any fingerprints on the tape now, except for yours, of course," Nancy said to him, "but don't handle the cassette any more. Maybe the kidnapper got sloppy and the police will be able to pick up some other prints on it."

"Okay," Lenny said, his cheeks coloring a little. "I should've been more careful after I played the tape the first time."

"Okay, so we know the tape was hand-delivered," Nancy said. "When?"

"Bess and I listened to yesterday's tapes in the late afternoon," Lenny said. "It would've been sometime after that."

"Who could've slipped into the station and left the tape without anyone seeing him?" Nancy asked.

"Or her?" Lenny said.

"I suppose it could've been anyone," Nancy said. "Certainly during the commotion caused by the fire, someone could've planted the tape without anyone noticing. Everyone at the station was busy concentrating on Jim Flagg and the fire in the basement." She sighed. "I suppose that still leaves Jim Flagg as a suspect. He could've planted it before the fire."

116

Nancy thought a moment and turned to Neal Graham. "How about during the night? Is the station locked up after everyone leaves?"

"Well," Neal Graham said, "of course, not everyone leaves. There is a deejay on duty after eleven, as well as an engineer. And all of the employees have keys to the station."

"So we're back to square one," Lenny said. "Anyone at the station could be the person we're looking for."

"Well, I guess I'd better go call the police and have them take charge of this tape. Then I have to see about getting that ransom money together," Graham said. A worried frown creased his forehead.

Just then Helena appeared in the doorway.

"What's happening with Jim Flagg?" she asked. "Has he talked yet?"

"I'm afraid not," Nancy said.

"He's being arraigned in criminal court today," Neal Graham said. "They're going to formally charge him with the kidnapping of Dan Wildman."

"Oh, no!" Helena covered her mouth with her hand and sank back against the door frame.

"The police and fire officials are investigating the fire in the basement before they file formal charges against him for arson or attempted murder," Graham added.

Nancy shook her head sadly. "I don't know exactly what happened last night with Flagg," she said, "but I'm convinced he didn't intend to kill me!"

"Of course not!" Helena said. "He isn't capable of that!"

"But what was he doing?" Lenny asked. "Why did he lock you up in the tool room? It just doesn't make sense."

"Maybe he was distracted," Helena said. "Maybe he was thinking about his wife and he didn't realize that the door would lock automatically."

"That's possible," Lenny said. "Jim certainly hasn't had his mind on his work lately."

"I've got to see about raising that ransom money," Graham said. "Helena, I'll call in after a while to see if there are any new developments. Hold down the fort."

"Right," Helena said, as Neal left the room.

"I think I'll stop by the hospital to see Mrs. Flagg," Nancy said. "Maybe she'll be able to tell me something that Jim is holding back."

She said goodbye to Helena and Lenny and headed out to her car. She opened the driver's door and slid in behind the steering wheel.

She found her keys at the bottom of her shoulder bag and turned the ignition.

Instantly, a voice blared out over the car speakers. Nancy instinctively reached to turn off the radio, but realized then that it wasn't on. The little red light next to the cassette player was on.

The voice was on tape, and it was repeating her name!

"Nancy Drew! Nancy Drew," it called. "I'm watching you, Nancy Drew. Too bad old Jim Flagg can't give you a clue!"

13

The Truth About Jim Flagg

Nancy was more puzzled than scared. What was the speaker trying to tell her? She rewound the tape and listened to it again. When the message had finished, the tape popped out of the cassette player a little. Nancy recognized the brand of tape. She'd seen that brand less than an hour ago in Lenny's office.

The tape was obviously from one of the kidnappers. Nancy couldn't recognize the speaker's voice. Someone had tampered with it electronically to make sure that the speaker could not be identified.

Nancy left the tape in the car's cassette player.

Maybe the police would be able to find finger-prints on it. She'd drop it off at the police station later.

She shifted the car into reverse and backed out of her parking space. Then she headed toward the hospital. She played the tape again several times as she drove.

"I'm watching you, Nancy Drew," the voice said. *"Too bad old Jim Flagg can't give you a clue."*

The speaker had said, *"I'm* watching you." Did that mean there had been only one kidnapper?

Nancy continued to think about the message. It seemed as if it was meant to scare her. But it was also taunting her. It was almost as if the speaker were *daring* her to keep going, to solve the case by steering her investigation away from Jim Flagg.

Why would he do that?

Nancy pulled into the hospital parking lot and guided her car into the nearest space. She entered the hospital and asked the receptionist where she could find Mrs. Flagg's room. Within minutes she was standing outside of room 340.

The door was slightly open.

"Mrs. Flagg?" Nancy peeked into the room.

The drapes at the window were open and there were cheerful bouquets of flowers on the ledge.

In the bed lay a tiny, pale woman with gray

hair. She was dressed in a pink nightgown and at the moment was peering worriedly over her glasses at Nancy.

"Mrs. Flagg?" Nancy repeated, stepping into the room.

"Yes? Oh. When the door opened, I was hoping you'd be my husband," she said. "Are you a hospital volunteer?"

"No," Nancy said. "My name is Nancy Drew. I'm doing some work for KRCK. I spoke with your husband this morning and I wanted to see you."

"Is he all right?" she asked anxiously. "He usually calls first thing in the morning before he comes over. But I haven't heard from him at all today. And he didn't call last night, the way he usually does."

Nancy thought a moment before answering. Obviously, Mrs. Flagg didn't know that her husband was in jail. It was probably for the best. Worry would not help her to get well.

"Oh, he's fine," Nancy said. "I think he's busy at the moment." Busy worrying about his wife, Nancy thought.

Mrs. Flagg smiled a little and shook her head. "What a dear man I married," she said. "Why, he's been here every day, sometimes two or three times, to see me."

"He's very concerned about you," Nancy said.

"I know," Mrs. Flagg said. "He shouldn't worry so much. It's not good for his health, you know."

Nancy smiled.

"And I'm worried about his work at the station," Mrs. Flagg said. "He's *here* so much, I'm afraid that he's going to lose his job. I tried to talk to him about it, but he just won't listen."

"Did he tell you he wasn't supposed to leave?" Nancy asked.

"He didn't have to," Mrs. Flagg said. "He's worked at **KRCK** for nearly twenty years. He was never able to come home during his work hours." She paused. "No, I think Jim has been leaving without telling anyone. I know Neal Graham— he would never give Jim permission to leave so often."

Nancy agreed with her silently.

"That nice Dan Wildman usually covers for Jim, I think," Mrs. Flagg said.

"I'm sure he does," Nancy said, realizing that Mrs. Flagg must not know about the kidnapping either.

"How are you feeling, Mrs. Flagg," Nancy asked gently.

"Oh, pretty well," she answered bravely. "The doctors are wonderful, but—well, everything is so expensive. Jim says not to worry, but I don't know. All these medical bills . . ." She looked up at Nancy sharply. "But don't you say a word to Jim! I told him everything is all right."

"I won't," Nancy promised. "I'm sure that it will all work out, Mrs. Flagg. Everyone at the station is thinking about you and wishes you a fast recovery."

"Thank you, my dear," Mrs. Flagg said. She put out her hand. "I appreciate your visit. Maybe Jim decided to put in some extra time at work—to make up for being here during work hours."

"You may be right," Nancy said, taking Mrs. Flagg's hand. "It was good to meet you. I'll tell Jim I saw you."

Nancy left Mrs. Flagg's room more convinced than ever that Jim Flagg was not involved in the kidnapping of Dan Wildman. But she felt frustrated that she didn't seem to be able to prove his innocence. She passed the nurses' station at the end of the hall. A round-faced woman in a white uniform waved to her.

"Were you visiting Mrs. Flagg?" the woman asked. She rounded the large semicircular desk and walked toward Nancy.

"Yes," Nancy answered.

"Is that her husband we've been hearing about on the news?" the nurse asked.

"Yes, I'm afraid so," Nancy replied. "I guess the story has been getting a lot of attention."

"Did you tell her about the kidnapping and her husband's arrest?"

"No," Nancy said. "That would only worry her."

The nurse looked relieved. "Oh, good. Mrs. Flagg's condition is not very good, I'm afraid. Any bad news could certainly harm her health."

Nancy thought a moment. "I'm glad you stopped me. Mrs. Flagg said her husband has spent a great deal of time here. Is that true?"

"Oh, yes," said the nurse. "I've never seen a husband more devoted to his wife. He's here all the time."

"Do you remember if he was here on Sunday evening between six and seven?"

The woman frowned and stared at the floor. "Let's see. That's the patients' dinner hour. I was on duty then. Hmmm." Then she looked up. "Yes, he was here. I remember because Mrs. Flagg's favorite television program is on at that time and her husband is always here to watch it with her."

Nancy smiled broadly. "That's just what I was hoping to hear."

"And if Mr. Flagg parked in the hospital parking lot, his parking validation will confirm it," the nurse said. "It will have the date and time on it."

Nancy grinned broadly. "That's the best news

125

I've ever heard! Thanks!" she exclaimed to the startled nurse.

She hurried to her car. Jim Flagg was innocent —without a doubt.

"But," Nancy said to herself as she drove out of the parking lot, "if he isn't the kidnapper—*who is?*"

14

Cornering a Kidnapper

Nancy drove toward the police station trying to suppress the rush of excitement that was welling up inside of her.

So Jim Flagg had been at the hospital at the time of the kidnapping! Nancy now had a witness to that. And if Jim had kept the parking validation, she would, without a doubt, be able to prove to the police that he was innocent.

Nancy handed the tape she'd found in her car to the desk sergeant, who promised to give it to Chief McGinnis. Then she asked to see Jim Flagg, and was ushered into the same small room they'd used earlier.

"I can't stop thinking about my wife," he said.

He hung his head. "She doesn't know where I am."

"I stopped at the hospital to see her," Nancy said. She placed her hand over his on the table. "I didn't tell her where you are."

Flagg looked up anxiously. "How is she?"

"She's doing pretty well," Nancy said. "But she's worried about you."

Flagg said nothing, but stared at the floor.

"Mr. Flagg," Nancy said carefully, "you didn't want to defend yourself to the police, but you weren't at the radio station when Dan was kidnapped, were you?"

Flagg tensed but said nothing.

"You couldn't have kidnapped Dan," she continued, "because you were at the hospital then, with your wife."

Flagg let out a long sigh. "Yes. Did my wife tell you?"

"No," Nancy said. "A nurse at the hospital told me she remembered that you were watching television with your wife when the kidnapping took place."

"Yes, I was," Flagg said. "Dan Wildman always covered for me so I could be with Mandy." He paused. "Dan's a real nice guy. He knew it was important that I go and cheer her up, so he always let me go. Of course, I'd have asked Mr. Graham for permission, but he'd never have

128

allowed it. I didn't have a choice. I *had* to sneak out so I could see Mandy and keep up her spirits."

"I know she appreciates how much you care about her," Nancy said.

"Graham would fire me now if he found out about it. Dan told me not to tell Graham. He said I'd probably lose my job. He said this was just between me and him."

"He told you that?" Nancy asked in a surprised tone.

Flagg nodded. "That's why I didn't tell the police where I was," he said. "I figured they'd tell Mr. Graham and I'd get fired. And that would be terrible." He gazed directly at Nancy. "I need my job, Ms. Drew. I need all the money I can get. Are you going to tell Mr. Graham what I did?"

"No," Nancy said. "I don't think it's going to be necessary to tell him."

Flagg looked at her quizzically.

"For one thing, I think you're going to be out of jail by tomorrow morning," Nancy said with a smile. "Especially if you have a hospital parking validation."

Flagg nodded. "It's in the glove compartment of my car."

Nancy smiled at him. "Then you're a free man, Mr. Flagg. In fact, I think I just solved this whole case."

Jim Flagg looked at her, astonished. "What?"

"I think I have a hunch about who's *really* behind the kidnapping of Dan Wildman."

Nancy hurried upstairs to Chief McGinnis's office. Quickly, she told the chief what she had discovered about Jim Flagg. The chief promised to look into the situation.

Nancy left the station and headed home. She called Lenny at the radio station and told him she'd be coming down there later that evening. "Meet me in the lobby with Tom Cottner. I want to try an experiment," she told Lenny. "If it works, I may be able to wrap up this case!"

Nancy arrived at KRCK just after nine o'clock that night. The parking lot was nearly deserted, and the moon cast an eerie glow over the brick building. Nancy shuddered. The place didn't look very friendly in the gloom of night.

Lenny and engineer Tom Cottner were waiting for her in the lobby. Lenny bounded over to her, grinning, as soon as she entered. "What's the plan, Nance—I mean, Nancy? Whatcha got up your sleeve?"

"Thanks, both of you, for meeting me here," Nancy said. "I have an idea that might—just *might*—flush out the kidnapper. But I need your help."

"We'd do anything you ask, wouldn't we, Tom?" Lenny said.

Tom smiled a little and held up his palms. "Hey, I'm here, right?"

"Come with me," Nancy said.

Tom and Lenny followed Nancy to the announcer's booth. Through the window they could see Ray leaning back in his chair, his arms folded over his chest, listening to the music he was playing.

Nancy opened the door. "Mind if we come in?" she asked.

"Not at all," Ray said. "I'm playing a whole album now. Anyway, you three are probably the only audience I'll have all night."

"What do you mean?" Nancy asked.

Ray made a face. "Nobody listens at this hour."

"But this is the top spot," Lenny protested. "All the kids listen to the radio while they do their homework."

Ray shrugged.

Nancy spoke up. "Ray, I'd like to try an experiment."

"Nancy thinks it'll draw out the kidnapper!" Lenny burst out. Then he said, more quietly, "Am I right, Nancy?"

Nancy smiled. "You're right on target, Lenny."

"Whoa," Ray said. "What are you talking about?"

"I'd like to make a tape," Nancy said, "announcing that Dan Wildman has been found."

"Wow!" Lenny said. Tom looked at Lenny and rolled his eyes.

"Why would I want to do that?" Ray challenged.

"I have a hunch the kidnapper will be listening. What you say will force him to come out in the open," Nancy said, sounding more certain than she felt. "If I'm right, our kidnapper is the type of person who won't be able to resist showing up. He'll want to let everyone know how clever he's been."

"And what if it doesn't work?" Tom asked.

"Then we say later that the announcement was based on a false report turned into the station. We wouldn't need to explain more than that."

Ray considered this. "I don't know," he said doubtfully.

"Hey, what have we got to lose?" Lenny said, waving his arms with enthusiasm. "I like it!"

Ray and Tom looked at each other a moment. Just then the album playing on the air was over.

"Hold on," Ray said, holding up a finger. He turned to the console and flicked a switch. "And that," he said into the microphone, "was the number-one album across the country this week."

He paused a moment before he spoke again. "And now for a treat. I hope you like Springsteen, because I have a string of his hits to play for you now. Uninterrupted. Coming up next."

He picked up a cart, slapped it into the machine over the console, and poked a button. Instantly, a commercial for a local grocery store came on.

Lenny grinned at Nancy. "He's going to do it for you!" he whispered. "Running a string of uninterrupted songs will free him for a while."

Ray handed Nancy a piece of paper and a pencil.

"Write what you want me to say," Ray said.

Nancy wrote the message.

When the commercial was over, Ray picked up a cartridge from a shelf next to him and pushed it into the machine. Instantly, Bruce Springsteen's voice filled the room. Ray turned down the volume so the tape couldn't be heard.

Nancy handed the "script" back to Ray. He read it and nodded.

"Okay, let's lay one down," he said. "We'll do it right here."

He turned to another machine and pushed a new tape into the recording slot. He poked a button and read.

"I have some great news for Dan Wildman fans! Word has just come in," he said, holding the paper up in front of his face, "that Dan the Wild Man has been found! That's all I can tell you at the moment. We'll keep you informed of any further developments. I repeat, Dan the Wild Man has been found!"

He pushed the Stop button and turned to Nancy.

"How was the reading?"

"Great!" she said.

"You want to keep this take?"

"Yes, I liked it," she said.

Ray popped the tape out of the machine and handed it to her.

"What now?" he asked.

"I want to wait until around ten o'clock and then put it out over the air," she said.

"What do you think will happen?" Ray asked.

"I don't know," Nancy said. "But if the kidnapper is listening, I think he might make a move."

"Toward the station?" asked Lenny, wide-eyed. "While we're here?"

"That's what I'm hoping," Nancy said.

Nancy turned to Lenny and Tom. "I'll meet you both in the lounge in a minute," she said. "I need to talk to Ray alone."

Lenny and Tom nodded and left the booth.

"What's up?" Ray wanted to know.

"There's just one more thing I'd like you to do with one of those cartridges," she told him.

She explained the second part of her plan. Then she left the booth and headed for the pay phone in the lobby. After making a quick phone call to Chief McGinnis, she went back to relax with Lenny and Tom in the lounge until it was time for Ray to play their taped message. The three drank cans of soda and passed around a bag of stale potato chips from the snack machine.

Tom leaned back in his chair so that the front legs tipped off the floor.

"You know," he said to Nancy, "I didn't trust you at first. But you've really stuck with this. I wouldn't be surprised if you really solve this case."

Nancy smiled. "Thanks, Tom, but maybe you'd better hold your judgment until this one is wrapped up."

"Oh, you'll solve this case, all right!" Lenny said. "You always do!"

"Well, let's hope the kidnapper is listening," Nancy said, "and takes the bait."

"We'll find out soon enough," Tom said, checking the clock on the wall.

At a few minutes before ten, the three moved back into the announcer's booth.

"I think now would be a good time," Nancy said, handing Ray the tape. "Let's air the announcement."

At the end of the next song, Ray pushed the tape into the machine. They listened as Nancy's phony message went out over the air. After it was over, Ray put on some old Beatles music.

"Let's see what happens now," Nancy said, and they sat down in the cramped announcer's booth to wait.

"The red light over the console will flash if someone calls in," Lenny told Nancy. "The phone doesn't ring so it won't disturb the show."

"Don't hold your breath," Ray said. "As I said before, no one is listen—"

Before he had even finished his sentence, the red light flashed on.

"Ha!" Lenny said, grinning as he slapped his leg. "No one is listening, huh?"

Ray grabbed up the phone receiver. "KRCK," he said. He paused. "Yes, that's right. The report we got is that Dan has been found." Another pause. "No, I don't know any more about it. Yes. Well, thank you for calling."

As soon as he put down the receiver, the red light flashed again.

"Well, at least two people are listening," he said. He picked up the phone. "KRCK . . . Yes, you heard right. He's been found. We'll report any more news that we get over the air." He paused a moment. "Well, thank you. I'm glad you like the show. . . . You like this show as well as the Wild Man's?" Ray grinned. "Well, thank you, those are words I like to hear! Yes, goodbye."

"It seems you're more popular than you thought," Nancy said, smiling.

Ray put down the phone and the red light

flashed again. This caller also mentioned how much she liked Ray's show and how happy she was that Dan had been found. Ray turned from the phone looking happier than Nancy had ever seen him.

"This is really something!" he said. "People must really like this show!"

The calls came in nonstop for nearly an hour. Ray was obviously very pleased at the response.

But there was no word from the kidnapper.

"I guess I was wrong," Nancy said, glancing at the clock on the wall. "I thought he would have showed up by now."

Ray smiled ruefully. "Well, I for one am glad you did," he said. "Now I know that I'm appreciated. How many calls do you suppose I had?"

"Thousands!" Lenny said, exaggerating as usual.

Nancy stood up and stretched. "Well, I guess I'll go on home. I think the kidnapper would've made his move by now if he'd been listening."

She said goodbye and headed down the darkened hallway and into the lobby where there was no light at all. The corner couch and chairs huddled in the shadows, and Nancy shivered.

Stop it, she told herself. There's no reason to be jumpy. No one is here but the guys in the announcer's booth. The kidnapper probably hadn't even been listening.

She moved toward the door, but just before

reaching for the knob, she stopped short. Someone outside was trying to turn the knob!

Nancy moved back into the hallway and
peeked around the corner. She heard a soft jangle
of keys and then the click of metal as the person
on the other side slid a key into the lock.

Nancy's heart skipped a beat. She tiptoed
quickly back to the announcer's booth.

"Nobody move," she declared breathlessly.
"Someone's coming!"

15

The Case Is Solved

"Tom, Lenny, hide behind the equipment," Nancy directed. "Ray, continue with your show."

Nancy joined them out of sight on the floor and waited. Behind the equipment on the floor, Nancy heard the door open to the announcer's booth.

Ray cried out in surprise. "But what are you doing here?" Ray asked.

Before Nancy could stop him, Lenny leaped out from behind the equipment and jumped on the intruder.

"I've got you!" he yelled. "Hey!" Then he laughed and shouted. "It's *you!* You're all right!"

Nancy and Tom stood up.

"I can't believe it," Tom said.

Standing just inside the doorway was Dan Wildman!

Lenny laughed. "You're safe! You're safe!" He was so excited, he began jumping up and down. "What happened, Dan? Did you escape from the kidnapper? How did you get away? Where did they hold you?"

"Yeah, I got away," Dan said, laughing. "And now I'm back." He grinned at Ray Ludlow. "Glad to see me, Ray?"

"Of course, I'm glad to see you," Ray said. "We were all worried about you."

"But who kidnapped you, Dan? Where did they take you?" Lenny asked excitedly.

Dan didn't answer. He picked up a pair of headphones and turned them over and over in his hands.

"Why don't you tell them what really happened, Dan," said Nancy.

"What are you talking about, Nancy?" asked Tom.

Dan put the headphones down and looked at Nancy. "You knew, didn't you?" he said.

Lenny looked baffled. "Knew what?"

Nancy nodded, watching Dan steadily. "Dan was never kidnapped, Lenny."

"What?"

"Isn't that right, Dan?" she said.

Dan didn't respond.

"Dan is a very ambitious guy," Nancy explained. "Ambitious and greedy for fame. He wanted the top night spot, the spot that belonged to Ray Ludlow. He decided that if he were kidnapped, the story would get lots of media attention—which it did."

Dan smiled. "It sure did. My face was plastered over every paper in the state. I'm famous."

"I can't believe this," Lenny said.

"Is it true, Nancy?" asked Ray.

Nancy nodded. "Dan knew that after the so-called kidnapping, he might even be more popular than you, Ray, and he could take your show away from you. All the people who followed the kidnapping would continue to listen to him on the air after his return. He knew he'd have a huge audience when he came back."

"He sure would," Lenny said.

"And then there was the possibility that another, larger station might be watching the story and hire him away from KRCK," Nancy said.

"That's what all deejays hope for," Tom said.

Nancy glanced again at Dan. "Am I getting it right so far, Dan?"

Dan was watching her, a little smile spreading slowly across his face.

"Right so far," he said. "Keep going. I like to hear how smart I am. It's the next best thing to being the most popular deejay around."

Nancy ignored Dan's conceited comments. She turned to Ray. "At first I thought that Neal

Graham or maybe even you, Ray, had staged the kidnapping."

"I know you suspected me," Ray said. "But I could never understand why. And why did you suspect Neal Graham?"

"For the same reason," Nancy explained. "For the publicity. But a couple of things tipped me off that it was Dan."

Dan's eyebrows shot up. "And what were they?" he asked, a trace of contempt in his voice.

"The cassettes. Remember the tape you left in my car's cassette player? The message was a silly poem. You might as well have signed your name all over it! Who else would've sent me a message in rhyme? It eventually made me wonder if you *wanted* to be found out. That's why I decided to try this little experiment."

Dan's face didn't change. He continued to smile a little, but said nothing.

Nancy continued. "And the cassette you left for Lenny to find, the one saying that we should get the ransom money together. It was the same brand of tape as the one left in my car. That made me think the same person planted both of them."

"Boy, you sure are sharp, Nancy!" Lenny said.

Nancy turned back to Dan. "Yesterday, I listened again to the tape of the alleged kidnapping. You could have prerecorded the 'kidnapping,' complete with noises of a struggle. I'll bet you were long gone when that went out over the air, weren't you?"

Dan laughed. "Do you think I'd have taken a chance on getting caught?"

"No, I don't," Nancy said. "You planned the whole thing very carefully. In fact, the tape fooled everyone, including the police. You did a good job."

Dan bowed, grinning. "Thank you."

"And that's what gave me the idea to make a phony tape for *you* to hear," Nancy said.

"Tonight's tape saying that I had been found. I don't like being caught at my own game." Dan frowned.

"Maybe you aren't as smart as you think you are," Ray said.

"You can say that again!" Lenny said. He stared at Dan, his former hero, and then sank into a chair. "I can't believe you did all that just to get famous."

"Wouldn't you have done it?" Dan asked severely. Then his mouth twisted in a smile. "That is, if you'd *thought* of it?"

"No," Lenny said seriously. "No, I wouldn't. Especially when a nice guy like Jim Flagg had to take the rap for what I'd done." Lenny gazed up at Dan. "How could you let that happen?"

Dan, once again, became quiet.

"Jim Flagg provided the final clue," Nancy

said. "When he admitted that he was visiting his wife in the hospital that night, the pieces seemed to fit together. He couldn't have been the kidnapper. And the other employees weren't here."

Dan's gaze on Nancy was hard. He was beginning to look angry.

"You knew that Helena was in Graham's office the way she always is at that time. You sent Jim Flagg to the hospital and sent Tom to the lounge for a cigarette—"

"He'd sent me out, too," Lenny said. "For an ice cream sundae. Only I got back early, so you sent me to the station library. But there's something you didn't know. I came back right away."

"What do you mean?" Dan asked.

"I forgot my key. When I came back to get it, I saw Jim Flagg." Lenny turned to Nancy. "Or, I thought I did."

Nancy nodded. "But it was Dan. You were disguised, weren't you, Dan?" Nancy asked. "You were dressed as Jim Flagg. Lenny walked by and all you saw was his back. But it was *you* in the announcer's booth!"

Dan's face didn't change.

Nancy continued. "Dan knew that Jim always wore those same gray work clothes with heavy leather shoes. He put them on just in case someone like you came by, Lenny.

"Then you went back to the announcer's booth and put on the prerecorded tape of your 'abduction,' " Nancy said. "And walked out still dressed as Jim Flagg."

Now Dan smiled. He threw up his hands. "Well, I've got to hand it to you," he said dramatically, taking center stage. "You figured it all out. Every last bit of it."

"So where have you been?" Lenny asked, rising from his chair. "Where were you while everyone worried about you and wondered if you would make it out alive?"

Dan smiled. "I have a little cabin just outside of River Heights along the river."

Lenny folded his arms and looked at Dan with disgust. "Great," he said. "Just great."

"Yeah," Dan said. "It *is* great. I've got a radio and TV there, too."

"So you kept informed about everything that was happening," Nancy said.

"You bet I did."

"And you phoned the papers from a telephone booth to tell them that a ransom note had been received by KRCK."

"Well," Dan said, "I had to make sure that the media would find out. I didn't know whether Graham would tell them."

"What I don't get," Lenny said, "is what was going to happen after you picked up the ransom money. How was all of this supposed to end?"

"Easy," Dan said. "I was going to 'escape' from the horrible kidnappers—after having gotten hold of the ransom money—and return myself and the money to the station. To a hero's welcome, of course."

Lenny just stared. "Maybe even a ticker-tape parade," he said sarcastically. Then he sighed. "Well, I've got to hand it to you, Dan. It was brilliant."

Dan laughed. "Yes, it was, wasn't it?"

He looked at Nancy, a nasty gleam in his eyes. "But now that you know the whole story, I can't let you go and tell everyone."

He reached into his pocket and pulled out a gun.

Tom and Lenny gasped.

"Listen, Dan," Nancy said carefully. "You haven't done anything really harmful. Why don't you just put the gun down and give yourself up. If you turn yourself in now, I'm sure the authorities will go easy on you."

"Turn myself in! Are you kidding? No, I've come this far," Dan said. "I'm not turning back now. My career is at stake."

"You'd kill us for your career?" Lenny asked, gaping at Dan.

"Of course," Dan said, grinning. "I'm going to be a star!"

Lenny lunged for the gun but tripped and landed facedown at Dan's feet. Dan stepped back in surprise, and Tom jumped at Dan. He knocked Dan on the floor, and they rolled over in the small

146

room, grappling for the gun, which had slid over near Nancy's feet.

Nancy reached for it, but before she had it in her grasp, Dan grabbed it away from her.

"Don't move, any of you," Dan said evenly. "It's my show now."

16

Wrap-up

A hush fell over the room.

Finally, Nancy spoke. Her voice was calm and quiet. "Dan, this doesn't make sense."

"Stand up," Dan said. "I don't *want* to hurt you, but you figured it out. I can't let you turn me in."

Nancy got to her feet.

"What are you going to do with us?" Lenny asked.

"Well, you don't give me much of a choice, do you?" Dan said nastily.

Ray leaned back on the console and reached behind his back. Dan saw his movement and jumped.

"What are you doing?" he asked.

"It's all over, Dan," Ray said. "We're on the air."

A look of horror passed over Dan's face. "For how long?"

"Ever since you walked in here," Ray said. "Nancy knew you'd come tonight. She told me to be ready. There's a cart in the machine there, but it's not playing."

The red light over the console lit up.

"Look, now we're even getting phone calls from our audience," Ray said evenly. He gestured toward the phone. "Do you want to answer them?"

Dan glanced around him, threw the door open and bolted into the hallway.

Nancy ran down the hall after him. Just as she reached the lobby, Dan opened the station door and took several running steps down the sidewalk.

"Stop! Police!" voices shouted at him.

Dan dropped his gun, froze where he was, and then slowly raised his hands over his head. "Don't shoot," he said. "I give up."

Neal Craham stood at the end of the long table at Reece's, an elegant restaurant at the edge of River Heights. Behind him were large glass windows overlooking the river and the woods on the far bank. The trees along the river were edged in the red light of the sun, which was sinking below the horizon.

"Well, it's over, thank goodness," Neal Graham said, raising a glass of champagne.

He looked at the people sitting around the table. Besides the employees at KRCK were Nancy, Bess, and George. "I'd like to thank you all for hanging in there with us during these last few days. I know it hasn't been easy for any of you."

"You can say *that* again!" Lenny said. He made the comment to Bess, who was seated next to him, but everyone at the table heard his remark, and they laughed.

"It's tough when your heroes disappoint you, I know," Graham said in Lenny's direction. "But I'd like to concentrate on some positive thoughts tonight," he continued. "Nancy, would you mind standing up?"

Nancy blushed but stood up.

"This young woman really surprised me," Graham said. "Of course, I'd read all about her in the papers, but I didn't expect that she could solve our mystery for us. I thought she was too young, too inexperienced. But she certainly proved me wrong."

Nancy smiled. "I had a lot of help," she said, "but thank you."

"You're too modest!" Tom shouted from the

other end of the table. The diners nodded in agreement and smiled as Nancy sat down.

"Someone else in this room surprised me, too," Graham said. "I thought Lenny Gribble was too young and immature to be of much use around the station." He turned to the young man and smiled. "But now I know what a valuable employee he is." Lenny grinned. "And thank you, Helena, for persuading me to give him a chance."

Helena smiled and nodded, accepting the compliment.

"Lenny," Graham said, "I'm moving you into Dan Wildman's spot."

"On the air?" Lenny asked, wide-eyed.

"That's right, kid," Graham said, grinning. "Think you can handle it?"

"Oh, wow, yes!" he said, rising from his chair in excitement. "I've got some *great* ideas! Just wait, I'll tell you about them tomorrow morning! Oh, man, this is really great, I can't believe it!"

Ray, sitting next to Lenny, reached up, put a hand on Lenny's shoulder, and pulled him down into his chair.

"Down, boy," he said. "You'll get your chance." Everyone laughed.

Graham turned and smiled at the man at his right. "Jim, I just want to tell you how very glad I am that this has been settled and how sorry I am that it had to involve you. You've been a hardworking, faithful employee of KRCK for many years, and I hope you'll be with us for many more. And I'd like to say in front of all these witnesses that we're going to set up a work schedule that lets you spend more time with your wife."

Flagg sat there, beaming with pleasure.

"After Dan disappeared," Graham said, addressing the whole group, "I offered a fifteen-thousand-dollar reward for information leading to Dan's return. It certainly didn't turn out the way I thought, since Dan 'kidnapped' himself, but I think it's only appropriate that the reward money go to Nancy Drew. I can't imagine how this would have turned out without her."

Everyone clapped, and Neal Graham handed Nancy a long white envelope.

Nancy took the envelope in surprised silence. After a moment, she said, "Thank you, Mr. Graham, but I could never have solved this case without the information that Mrs. Flagg gave me about Jim's visits to the hospital." She stood up at the table. "I think *she* really solved this case. So, Jim, I'd like to present this reward money to you and your wife with my thanks."

She handed him the money as the people at the table cried out in agreement and stood and applauded Jim Flagg. Flagg looked astonished, then took out a handkerchief and wiped his eyes. He accepted the envelope from Nancy, and smiled and nodded repeatedly at his friends.

"He'll be able to pay for his wife's medical

care," Bess whispered to Nancy. "Oh, Nancy, you are wonderful!"

While the group was still clapping, Jim leaned over to Nancy. "I can't tell you how sorry I am about the fire. I wasn't thinking straight, I was so anxious to get to Mandy at the hospital. I didn't realize I'd locked the door." He looked at the floor, ashamed. "I hope you believe me, Ms. Drew."

Nancy put a hand on his arm. "Of course I do."

After the noise died down, Lenny stood at his seat. He looked over the faces around him. "I think everybody needs heroes. Dan was always the person I most admired, and it was a real shock to find out that he wasn't the guy I thought he was. But I'm not too upset about it." He smiled at Nancy and turned back to the others. "I have a new hero now. Nancy Drew. And I'm her biggest fan!"

THE HARDY BOYS® SERIES By Franklin W. Dixon

Simon & Schuster, Mail Order Dept. HB5, 200 Old Tappan Rd., Old Tappan, N.J. 07675

Please send me copies of the books checked. Please add appropriate local sales tax.
☐ Enclosed full amount per copy with this coupon (Send check or money order only)
☐ If order is $10.00 or more, you may charge to one of the following accounts: ☐ Mastercard ☐ Visa
Please be sure to include proper postage and handling: 0.95 for first copy; 0.50 for each additional copy ordered.

Name _____

Address _____

City _____ State/Zip _____

Books listed are also available at your bookstore. Prices are subject to change without notice.   657-10